"Maybe you just need a break from it all. There's been a lot to deal with."

"Maybe."

"No maybe about it," Wyatt said. "You were awfully clinical when you called me and told me you were in a mess."

She gazed into his face, reading his concern but more, his kindness. He'd always accepted her just as she was, and he was doing it right now.

He touched her cheek, and a pleasant shiver ran through her. Well, at least she could still feel that. It would have been so easy to just fall into his arms. Because she wanted to know what it would feel like to rest her head on his shoulder. To feel his lips on hers. To feel his skin against hers. To feel him filling the emptiness inside her.

She'd always wanted to know.

CONARD COUNTY: THE NEXT GENERATION

Dear Reader,

Judge Wyatt Carter had been wandering the back of my mind for some time. He's an attractive figure, and every time he popped to the foreground of my thoughts, I'd think, "Someday."

Well, Judge Carter's day finally came. He refused to be ignored any longer, but then he's a judge. To any who think he's an unusual judge, I'd like to assure you he's not. I've known judges very much like him, in and out of the courtroom. Despite what most of us see on TV and in movies, judges are human, caring and often kind when the situation warrants. And out of those robes...well, they can be fun, too.

When Wyatt's old friend from law school falls on troubled times, helping her comes as naturally to him as breathing. He's not one to care about gossip, and not particularly concerned about his upcoming reelection. It's enough that Amber needs him to help her through an unexpected pregnancy and the troubles it caused with her career.

Enjoy!

Rachel Lee

His Pregnant
Courthouse Bride

—

Rachel Lee

Recycling programs
for this product may
not exist in your area.

ISBN-13: 978-0-373-62327-3

His Pregnant Courthouse Bride

Copyright © 2017 by Susan Civil Brown

Printed in U.S.A.

www.Harlequin.com

Rachel Lee was hooked on writing by the age of twelve and practiced her craft as she moved from place to place all over the United States. This *New York Times* bestselling author now resides in Florida and has the joy of writing full-time.

Visit the Author Profile page
at Harlequin.com for more titles.

Prologue

Circuit Judge Wyatt Carter had just finished a pleasant dinner at home, a too-rare occurrence, because he lived alone and was generally too busy to take the time to indulge in cooking. But this was a quiet Sunday evening after a comfortable day of catching up on his reading, and he'd made the effort to cook chicken Alfredo for himself and enjoyed it with a glass of pinot grigio. He felt somewhat self-indulgent, but considering how little time he had for indulgences, he didn't feel guilty.

When the phone rang, he assumed it was his father. Earl Carter ran the family law practice, although lately it had shrunk because Earl was getting older and didn't take as many cases. Earl seemed content enough to let the practice contract even though he'd once said it was his legacy to his son. Then Wyatt had become a circuit court judge, and the plans of a father-son practice had melted away.

But it was not his father, much to his surprise. It was a voice out of the past.

"Wyatt?"

He recognized Amber Towers's voice. They'd kept in touch over the last decade, mostly by email and occasional phone calls. Amber had moved on from law school to a large firm in St. Louis, then recently to a much bigger firm in Chicago, headed for the heights. Wyatt, who had graduated two years ahead of her, had joined the military and spent three years in the judge advocate general's office. Then he'd come back to out-of-the-way Conard County to fulfill his father's dream of a shared practice.

He and Amber had once been very close friends, although nothing more than that, and since then they'd maintained a long-distance friendship, except for dinner or lunch at a bar association conference.

Now he heard her voice with astonishment, since she hadn't called in ages, and concern popped into his mind. "Amber? What's wrong?"

"You're never going to believe it. I'm in a mess. Got an hour or so?"

"Of course."

His mind dived down the byways of memory, recalling Amber as he had first seen her. She was young for a first-year law student, having gone to college two years early and finishing her bachelor's degree in three years.

She had, in short, been barely nineteen. He'd been twenty-seven, because he'd taken a couple of years after college to try his hand at other things before going to law school. She'd been very pretty, so pretty that every guy who wasn't already married—and some who were—chased her. He hadn't chased. It wasn't that he hadn't found her attractive, but facing his tour with the military in exchange for them paying his law school expenses, he felt it was the wrong time to get involved, especially since the direction she wanted to take was far from his path. He'd also felt that given the difference in their ages, it might be close to cradle robbing. Amber had seemed so young to him then.

So they'd become friends over textbooks and in oral arguments. He'd mentored her, having already taken the classes she was in, and she'd challenged him with her sharp mind.

A lovely woman barely emerging from adolescence, with dark hair, a pleasant figure and a face that had been pretty but painfully young. Of one thing he had been sure, though: Amber would rise to the top. He wouldn't have been surprised if she reached the Supreme Court.

But now she was in trouble?

He poured himself another glass of wine, carried it to his easy chair and prepared to listen.

It didn't take an hour, either. Amber was indeed in a mess.

Chapter One

"I think this is a bad idea," Earl Carter told his son, not for the first time in the last month.

"Amber needs a place to get her feet under her, Dad," Wyatt answered. The two men were sharing a beer at the kitchen table as they had so many times over the years.

"People will talk, a strange woman moving in with you."

"Dad, it's the twenty-first century."

Earl snorted. "Not in a lot of places in this county it isn't, Wyatt. Dang, you're a judge! Decorum and all that."

Wyatt hid a smile behind his beer bottle. Clearly Earl was one of those who hadn't quite come into the new century. But while he never would have admitted it to his father, he wasn't so sure about having Amber here, either.

First off, she was a city gal, and Conard City was barely a blip on the map. Secondly, they'd been friends in law school over ten years ago. A bunch of keeping-in-touch emails and an occasional phone call didn't mean he really knew the woman she had become. Nor could he know how all those years at huge law firms might have changed her.

"Maybe I should move back in," Earl said. He'd moved out after Wyatt had come back from his years with the judge advocate general's office, because— as he'd said at the time—he was tired of keeping up the huge old family house, and besides, what woman would want to marry a man who was living with his father?

"I don't need a chaperone," Wyatt said now.

"Maybe you need a headshrinker." Earl leaned back, his comfortable belly stretching his white shirt. He'd come directly from his law office, where he still wore a suit every single day. A Western-cut suit with a bolo tie, to be sure, but still a suit. He often evinced disapproval of his son's penchant for wearing jeans beneath his judicial robe. Of course, he voiced plenty of disapproval for Wyatt's motorcycle, too. "Look, son, it hasn't been that long since you broke it off with Ellie."

"What does Ellie have to do with it? That was over a year ago, and you know why I broke it off." Wyatt shifted irritably. "Any woman who expects me to dismiss charges against her cousin is a woman I don't want in my life."

"I get it. You were right, not saying you weren't. But that isn't the story she put around."

"So? What does that have to do with now?"

"Ellie's gonna make trouble, mark my words. Moving a big-city woman in with you?"

"Temporarily, Dad," Wyatt said with as much patience as he could muster. "It's nobody's business."

"You know better than that. You have an election coming up."

"Retention only. And if folks around here don't want me to be the judge anymore, you'll have a partner in that law practice again."

Earl sighed. "You never set your sights high enough."

Wyatt almost laughed. "I remember a time you thought that the practice of Carter and Carter was as high I needed to set my sights."

"But now you're a judge! You could become a district judge, maybe even go to the state supreme court."

Wyatt experienced a jolt of shock. He had never dreamed that his father envisioned that kind of future for him. It had been surprise enough when he'd been nominated to the bench as a circuit judge. Now this comment from a man whose highest ambition had once been to see his son's name on the shingle beneath his. "What got into you, Dad?"

Earl shrugged and took another swig of beer. "After you were nominated for the bench, I started wondering if I was holding you back." Then he winked. "Not that I want to see you taking off again. Hard enough when you were at school and in the military."

Holding the icy bottle in one hand, listening to the autumn wind picking up outside, Wyatt wondered if his dad was serious. He himself cherished no great ambitions that would carry him far away. He'd done that already, seen his share of the world with the JAG, and had decided things were just dandy here at home among people he'd known all his life. If he wanted adventure, that was what vacations were for. As it was, the daily parade of humanity that passed before his bench was entertaining and challenging enough, as was his work with youthful offenders.

"You should be thinking of these things," Earl said, returning to the whole point of his visit.

"I don't see a political future for myself, Dad. It's enough I can get away for a couple of weeks, that I can go hunting for a weekend or two in the fall…"

Earl snorted. "And when was the last time you brought home any meat?"

Wyatt stifled a grin. "Hunting is good for that image you're worried about. Someone from the city council or county commission asks me every year. I go to the dang lodge, drink with the boys, and I can't help it if I'm a lousy shot."

"You weren't always," Earl retorted, but a twinkle came to his eyes. Then his expression darkened again. "I know you're not going to listen to me. When's that woman arriving?"

"*Amber* is arriving some time this evening. Hang around and you'll meet her."

"And you're throwing a party for her, too?"

Wyatt smothered a sigh. He knew perfectly well his father wasn't this dense and that Earl was giving him a hard time. "Not a party, Dad. I'm having a few people over next weekend so she can meet some other women. I'm not around much, and maybe she can find some friends while she's here."

"Hmm." Earl drained the rest of his beer and tossed the bottle in the trash. "I think I'll head on back to my place. Maybe give Alma a call."

Alma was his father's latest interest, a woman in her midfifties with a warm smile and a nicely plump figure. Wyatt often thought that Earl hadn't moved out of the family house so that his son could date, but rather so Wyatt wouldn't cramp his father's style. Wyatt's mother had been gone for nearly thirty years, but Earl had never remarried. He had, however, enjoyed a series of relationships.

Apparently, he wasn't worried about appearances for himself. Wyatt just shook his head as his father grabbed his coat and left. Earl was no fool, obviously, but the way he'd been talking tonight? Wyatt wondered what was really behind it.

A short while later he stood at the front window, the large living room behind him, the lights out so he could see. Wind was ripping the last autumn leaves from the trees and sweeping them down the street.

No, Earl was no fool. So maybe he was right that having Amber here was a mistake. The thing was, Wyatt had never been one to turn away someone in need. Far from it. He always had an overwhelming desire to help.

Mistake or no mistake, Amber was going to have a place to stay while she sorted out her life and where she wanted to go from here. Because she was right: she was in a mess.

Amber Towers pulled into Conard City and wondered if she was about to drop off the map. It wasn't that the town was clearly small—she'd been in a lot of small towns in her life—but after driving so many miles with nothing on either side of the road except rangeland and mountains, it *felt* like the ends of the earth.

The streetlamps had come on, casting sharp shadows beyond the pools of light. From inside most of the houses came a golden glow that somehow seemed to beckon, promising warmth, shelter and friendliness.

Just an illusion, she told herself. Her GPS audibly guided her to Front Street and right up to Wyatt's door. She pulled up against the curb, not wanting to block him in his narrow driveway. Other cars scattered along the street told her that on-street parking wasn't forbidden here.

Then she sat, her engine running, wondering what exactly she was doing. But she'd been wondering that for a while now. The whole situation stank, starting with her own naive stupidity and ending with her here, at an old friend's house, unemployed and scared.

Yeah, she'd admitted she was scared. She'd never imagined that her rising boat and bright future could run aground. Certainly not this way. Not when everything had been going so well.

With both hands gripping the steering wheel, she continued to hesitate. Yes, she'd called someone who was totally outside her current circle, looking for objectivity and a true friend. Wyatt had sprung quickly to mind when she'd wanted a sounding board. Even back in law school, all those years ago, he'd been imbued with common sense, with a way of distancing himself that was excellent for a lawyer and something she'd had to learn. He could put feelings aside and see clearly.

So she had asked him to see clearly.

He had. He hadn't told her what to do, not even indirectly, but he'd managed to draw the situation for her in sharp lines and propose several options for dealing with it.

She had chosen this one, and as soon as she had he'd said, "Well, then, you'll need a place to stay while you make up your mind about what you want to do. I've got plenty of room."

That was Wyatt. Always ready to help, a quality she had always admired in him, a quality she'd seen him display repeatedly during that year they'd been in law school at the same time. She'd accepted, but now she wondered if she was taking advantage of him. Even as she had qualms, she knew why Wyatt had been the only person she had told about her situation. She could count on him. Always. Other friends in her life had been nowhere near as steadfast.

It remained, however, this was *her* problem, *her* mess, and moving in on him and his life, even by invitation, had probably been a selfish thing to do.

Finally she quit arguing with herself and switched off her ignition. If she felt she was disrupting his life, that she was in the way somehow, she could leave tomorrow or the next day. After all, she was traveling light, most of her belongings packed away in storage for some better future day.

At last she climbed out of the car. The wind felt a little like Chicago, although considerably drier. It nipped through her jacket and gray slacks like a familiar bite. Not that she'd had that long to get used to it.

She watched the leaves blowing down the street and wondered if her life were blowing away with them. Big mistake, big consequences, and in an instant everything was different. She'd been a fool. Maybe that was the thing hardest to forgive in herself.

The porch light flipped on. Wyatt had seen her. The house itself was mostly dark, but he must have caught sight of her from somewhere. A fan window over the front door spilled warm light, and stained-glass insets on the front door glowed with color. His home. Inviting her.

The front door opened. She recognized his figure immediately, tall and straight with broad shoulders and narrow hips.

"Amber?"

"Coming," she answered promptly, settling her purse over her shoulder. Her bags could wait. For later, for never—the next few hours would tell.

She strode up the walk, climbed three steps, crossed the wide covered porch and walked straight into his waiting arms.

She hadn't expected this hug, but it felt so good she simply accepted it and fought down unwanted tears of relief. He'd never hugged her like this before, warm and tight, and reality proved to be far better than her youthful imaginings. She wished she could stay there forever. All too soon, he let her go.

"Come inside," he said kindly. "It's getting cold out here."

The house was large, and the foyer bigger than she expected, designed in a very different age. A dark wooden staircase led to the upstairs, dark wood wainscoting lined the walls beneath walls painted Wedgwood blue and the floor itself was highly polished wood decorated with a few large oriental rugs.

But she was more interested in Wyatt himself. Time

had changed him some. His face had sharper lines and seemed squarer than she remembered from four years ago at that convention. She thought she saw flecks of silver in his nearly black hair. Age had filled him out a bit, but in all the right places. He wore a dark gray sweater and jeans and was walking around in his stocking feet.

He smiled. "Come get comfortable," he suggested, his dark eyes friendly. "You must be tired after all that driving."

He helped her out of her jacket and hung it and her purse on the wooden coat tree beside the door. Glancing around again, she felt as if she'd wandered into a museum.

"Somehow," she said, "I didn't imagine you living in a place like this."

"It's been in the family for nearly a hundred years. A white elephant, but one I can't let go of. Or should I say can't get rid of."

She laughed, feeling some of her tension ease. "I need to move around, if that's okay. I haven't been out from behind the wheel in five hours."

"Pushed it, huh?"

"Very definitely."

"Well, feel free to wander. Something to drink? Coffee, tea, cocoa or stronger?"

Stronger was out of the question now, although she would have loved a glass of wine. "Cocoa sounds great. Can I follow you around?"

"Be my guest."

How awkward, she thought. For both of them. All those years between, and a bunch of emails, a few phone calls and a couple of meetings didn't make up for it. And for all she'd recently bared her soul to him on the phone, being here still felt…like she didn't belong?

The kitchen had been modernized, a shock after the foyer. The appliances were all new, stainless steel, and there was even a dishwasher. What she guessed were the original wood cabinets had glass-paned doors outlined in fresh white. Countertops had been covered in light gray granite that matched a tile floor.

"This is beautiful," she said, taking it in. "Big." Big enough for a nice-size island and a matching table.

"I have a secret chef somewhere inside," Wyatt replied lightly. "He rarely gets the chance to come out and play, though. Too busy."

"I love to cook, too, but I hear you. Ninety-hour weeks and I usually wind up at some restaurant."

"Same here. Say, did anyone in law school ever warn you this profession wouldn't leave time for a life?"

She had to laugh because it was so true. "Powder room?"

"Under the staircase in the foyer. Can't miss it."

She walked back into that amazing area and found the half bath without any problem. It, too, had been modernized with pleasant wallpaper and fixtures of recent vintage. She paused in front of the mirror, however, and stared at her reflection, realizing she appeared gaunt.

God. This had taken a lot out of her, maybe more than she had realized. She finger combed her short dark hair and tucked the bob behind her ears, but of course that didn't hide the circles under her eyes, and she must have lost a few pounds. Desperate to look less like a corpse, she pinched her cheeks to bring some color into them. This couldn't be good for the child she carried.

It was not the first time she'd thought about that, but mostly she had skimmed over it. Now she faced it, and felt her knees weakening. It was real, all of it was real, and the cloak of numbness she'd been wearing much of the time since everything had blown up simply vanished.

No longer an intellectual exercise, no longer a problem of humiliation, no longer a situation to be solved. It was her and the child growing inside her and nobody else. The reality was stark, the road ahead invisible.

A mess? It was more than a mess. She'd exploded her entire life into little pieces.

Chapter Two

Amber had headed to bed right after the cocoa. Wyatt had brought her suitcases in and showed her to the best guest room, then returned to his work before going to bed himself.

Last night had been uncomfortable, he thought as he made coffee in the morning and scrambled some eggs. They hadn't talked at all, except superficially and briefly about her trip, about the room that was to be hers. Strangers. It felt like two strangers. He hadn't really anticipated that. In his mind their friendship had remained as fresh as yesterday. Emails and other contacts didn't quite bridge the years. Nor did it help his sense of awkwardness to discover that he still found her every bit as attractive as he ever had.

But he was worried about her, too. The stress of the past weeks had clearly worked on her. He'd expected her to look a bit older than she had when he'd run into her at that conference four years ago, but not this pinched and drained. Worn. Her situation was awful, so maybe he shouldn't have been surprised.

He paused, looking out the window over the sink, noting that the wind was still blowing and leaves were still flying. By now, he thought with mild amusement, all the leaves in town should have been gone. But as he watched some of them eddy between the houses, he guessed they would hang around to be raked.

He heard steps behind him and turned to greet Amber. She looked a bit better this morning and was already dressed as if she were going to work in a navy blue pantsuit and white blouse. A bit much for hanging around the house.

"Well, good morning," he said with a smile.

She smiled back. "Sorry I was so dead last night."

"Long trip," he said. "Eggs? Toast? Coffee?"

"All of the above, please." She settled onto a stool on the far side of the island. "You have to work today, of course."

"I cleared most of my schedule for the week," he answered, turning back to the counter and cracking two more eggs into a bowl to whisk. "A few hours each day, rather than all day. Some hearings I can't avoid, and a trial that'll probably be over in a couple of hours after we finish jury selection."

"Can I come watch?"

"Of course." If she were in the courtroom with him, at least he wouldn't be wondering if she were sitting here feeling like hell and unable to do a damn thing about it.

He gave her a cup of coffee and the eggs he'd already cooked. "Dig in."

He started making his own eggs and heard her say, "You didn't have to clear your schedule for me."

"No, but I did anyway. You could have gone anywhere if solitude and four walls were all you wanted."

He was pleased to hear a quiet laugh from her. "Sadly true," she answered.

A minute later he carried his own plate and mug to the island and stood on the far side from her. "It's okay, Amber," he said before he started eating. "You're welcome here and we'll get over the awkwardness soon."

"I didn't expect it," she admitted. "In some ways I felt as if all these years hadn't passed."

"In some ways they haven't." He sipped his coffee. "But even back then we didn't share quarters."

That drew another laugh from her, a small one.

"Look, this place is practically a hotel. Just do whatever you need to in order to feel comfortable. Spend as much time or as little as you want with me. Make your own ground rules. I'm pretty adaptable."

She raised her face to smile at him. "Generous, too. Most of the problem is me, Wyatt. Everything is all messed up. Blown up. I feel as if I'm in a million pieces right now."

"Hardly surprising. You want to talk some more?"

"Maybe after court. You must need to go soon."

He glanced at the clock. Seven thirty. "Fifteen minutes. Can you be ready?"

"I *am* ready. But don't you need time to change?"

Wyatt looked down at his jeans and polo shirt. "No."

"Wow," Amber breathed. "I might like this place."

"Well, I do wear a robe. Most of the time."

The sound of the laughter that pealed out of her warmed his heart. If she could still laugh like that, then everything would be okay. For her.

Because suddenly, for him, he wasn't so sure. An attractive damsel in distress. Always his weak point, and more so for Amber.

The day was chilly and the wind whipped with ferocity. Amber almost felt like ducking as they left the house and walked to his car in the driveway. "Is this wind usual?" she asked once they were in the car.

"No. Usually we have a breeze, nothing bad, although it can get to be pretty constant if you get out onto the prairie. But here…" He shook his head as he turned over the ignition. "Some kind of front must be in the area, but I haven't looked at the weather."

"I was getting used to the wind in Chicago. I don't think it ever stops. But this is pretty with the leaves tossing in the wind."

"Until it comes time to rake," he answered.

"Will there be anything left?" she wondered as he wove their way down the street toward where she presumed they'd find the courthouse.

It was only a few blocks away, and she was instantly charmed. She'd half expected some functional building that had been erected recently, but instead saw a gorgeous older redbrick building with impressive columns sitting in a square filled with concrete benches and tables and the remains of summer flowers. And the statue of a soldier, watching over it all.

"Did they transplant this from New England?" she asked, amazed.

"The folks who built it wanted something to remind them of home, I guess. We have a church that looks like it was snatched out of the jaws of Vermont, too."

Amber was charmed. It might not be a large town, but what she had seen of it so far was gracious and inviting. Wyatt pulled around to the back of the courthouse and into a parking space labeled with his name: *Hon. Wyatt Carter.* Some of the other spaces had filled up, but they were all reserved—county attorney, court reporter and others.

"We finally emerged into the new century," he remarked after they climbed out and headed for the back door.

"Meaning?"

"We had to build a new jail outside town. It wasn't so long ago prisoners were kept in cells over the sheriff's office, but six cells is just about enough to dry out the drunks overnight. So…big jail. And I do a lot of my hearings over closed-circuit TV. No big deal to you, I'm sure, but it was a very big deal when we transitioned here."

She could almost imagine it. In a very short space of time he'd given her the feeling that this was an old Western town stepping very slowly into the modern era. She looked around just before he opened the door for her and saw that the entire square was surrounded by stores. She liked it.

She followed him into a narrow hallway painted institutional green with wood floors that creaked beneath their feet. They passed restrooms, the rear side of the county clerk's office, then climbed some equally creaky stairs to the second floor, where they entered his chambers.

The walls in the outer office were lined with books of statutes, something that must be left over from earlier days, she decided. Everyone relied on online research these days, and law libraries were available at the touch of a key if you had a subscription. They'd certainly done that in law school. But she looked around the walls, admiring the books, their solid look and feel. Two desks sat in the middle of all this magnificence.

"My reporter and clerk work there," he said.

Then they passed through to a chamber that was all dark wood, a massive desk and a few chairs. She thought she could detect old aromas of cigar smoke embedded in the walls. The only modernity was a multiple line phone and a computer.

"My home away from home," he said, glancing at his watch. "I've got a few minutes. Do you want to stay here or go into the courtroom?"

She'd been in a judge's chambers before, of course. It was inevitable for a lawyer. It didn't look like a place to browse, and she'd come to see him in court anyway.

"Courtroom," she answered decisively. A kind of tickled excitement awoke in her. She was going to see her old friend in the role of a judge. It was just cool enough to make her forget her other problems.

She walked through the door he pointed out and emerged in the courtroom, walking past the raised bench and past the attorney's tables, which were already occupied, ignoring the curious looks as she took a seat in the front row. She had no idea what was on his docket for today or whether the people waiting in the gallery with her were here to deal with legal problems or just to watch, but the place was filling rapidly.

The clock slipped past eight, almost as a courtesy to late arrivals, then a bailiff, in what appeared to be a deputy's uniform, called the court to order and announced Wyatt. "All rise. The Tenth District Circuit Court of the state of Wyoming is now in session, the Honorable Wyatt Carter presiding."

He came striding in, wearing a black robe, his jeans and boots flashing beneath it. She had to cover her mouth with her hand. She hadn't expected to enjoy this so much.

Wyatt tapped the microphone in front of him, and the thump came across the speakers. "All right," he said, looking out over the room. "Traffic court. Really, folks, don't you know better?"

And thus it began.

Amber was soon amazed. Wyatt didn't treat most of these people as if he just wanted them to pass out of his sight as soon as possible. He actually talked to them, and when he deemed it appropriate, he asked questions. He even postponed a few cases when the charges were serious and the accused claimed to be unable to afford an attorney. He promptly assigned them to the public defender on the spot.

"This is the second time you've come before this court for not having a driver's license," he said to a thirtysomething man in work clothes. "Didn't I order you to get a license last time?"

"Yes, sir."

"So why are you still driving without one?"

The man shuffled his feet. "I need to go to work."

Wyatt leaned back a little and studied the notes on his desk. "It says here you can't read. The state has an application for people who can't read. Why didn't you get one?"

"I tried."

At that Wyatt leaned forward. "What kind of work do you do?"

"I work at the ranches. Hired hand."

"No reading required for that, I suppose."

"No, sir."

"So why didn't you get a license?"

"I keep calling but they're busy. I can't even talk to someone. Always busy."

Wyatt turned to the clerk. "You get me the license people and you get this man an appointment with them before this day is over."

"Yes, Your Honor."

Wyatt turned back to the man in front of him. "Will you go to the test when my clerk tells you the time?"

"Yes, sir."

"You'd better. And I'm suspending your case pending your getting that license. Crap, can't get through?" He turned to the clerk again. "Let 'em know I'm not happy about this."

The clerk almost grinned. "Absolutely."

He looked at the man. "You stay here until she gets your appointment. And you'd better find somebody to drive you home, because you cannot drive without a license and I don't want to see you here again. Understood?"

Amber was amazed. Wyatt took a lot of personal interest, sometimes waiving fines when people simply couldn't pay them. But again and again, when something caught his attention, he zoomed in.

Then came the guy who was in front of him for the second time for driving on a suspended license.

"I told you to stop driving," Wyatt said. "What makes you think you can ignore the law like this? Your license was suspended for DUI. Now you're in front of me again for driving when you're not allowed to?"

The amusing part came after Wyatt ruled, telling the guy that the next time he was going to jail and was being spared this time only because he had small children to support. Then he added, "I'm leaving here in another few minutes, so you'd better find someone to drive you home. Because I'll recognize your face now and I'll chase you down and arrest you myself. Got it?"

Amber had never guessed that traffic court could be so fascinating and even moving. And Wyatt broke the mold.

Amber waited in the court after everyone had departed. She didn't feel free to just walk back into Wyatt's chambers. He might be dealing with something that was none of her business, or he might just be busy. She only waited about twenty minutes, though, before he entered the courtroom again, this time wearing his jacket and no robe and carrying a briefcase. "Free for the rest of the day," he said with a smile. "Do you want to go home or would you rather go down the block to the diner with excellent food and service that never comes with a smile?"

That surprised a little laugh from her. "Really?"

"Maude and her daughter are the local gorgons, but the food more than makes up for it."

"Then by all means the diner."

"Let's walk," he suggested, and this time they exited the courthouse by the grand front entrance. "I think these places were built to impress and intimidate," he said as they walked down the wide marble steps.

"I think you're right. It's a beautiful building."

"That it is. And you see the stone benches and tables scattered in the little park? When the weather allows we have people at nearly every one of them playing chess or checkers." He pointed. "Over there is the sheriff's office."

It looked like a regular storefront, which surprised her. "No Corinthian columns for him?"

Wyatt laughed. "None. They used to be in the courthouse basement a couple of generations ago, but then they needed more room and were getting squeezed out by the records and clerks. So they took up one side of the street there, and their offices run back inside behind the storefronts. Bigger than it looks from out here."

They crossed Main, which was right in front of the courthouse, to a side street where he pointed out other shops to her, one of them a craft shop in a house a little way past the diner, a dentist's office, a dress store, a bail bondsman and a couple of lawyers, one of them with the name Carter painted in gold letters on the window.

"Your father?" she asked.

"The same."

"So you practiced there for a while?"

"Yup." Then into the diner, which was quite busy. She couldn't miss the silence that fell suddenly as she walked in with Wyatt and felt like a bug under a microscope.

"Ignore it," he said under his breath. "They're just curious. Something new to talk about."

She hadn't considered that possibility. Being the subject of talk wasn't something she wanted, but then she reminded herself that she was only visiting. A week, two weeks, whatever, but eventually she was going to have to figure out the next path she needed to walk. And after what had happened in Chicago, she figured large law firms were off her list for some time. People gossiped there, too, and that gossip spread. For her it would be the kind of gossip that would make another firm leery of hiring her.

All of a sudden a man in a sheriff's uniform stood before them. He had a burn-scarred face and a gravelly voice. "Hey, Wyatt, we were just leaving. Take our booth."

Wyatt smiled and held out his hand to shake the other man's. "Amber, this is Gage Dalton, our sheriff. Gage, a lawyer friend of mine from Chicago, Amber Towers."

Gage's crooked smile was friendly as he shook Amber's hand. "Welcome to Conard City, Ms. Towers. If you decide you want to get out of town and visit a ranch, let me know. I've got several deputies who'd be glad to oblige. Or you can take a trail ride." He laughed. "Whole bunches of things to do, if you know where to look."

She met three more deputies as they departed, one of them a woman who had the same last name as a much older man with a Native American face. They didn't at all resemble each other, which raised her curiosity.

"The two named Parish," she began after they sat and the table had been cleared by a scowling woman.

"Micah Parish and his daughter-in-law, Connie."

Well, that explained a lot. "Family business, law enforcement?"

Wyatt flashed a grin. "Not exactly. Micah has a ranch, too, and his son, Ethan, left the sheriff's department to help out there. Unfortunately, I think we're going to see Micah retire before long. It'll be the end of an era."

"Meaning?"

Coffee cups slammed down in front of them and were filled by an older version of the woman who had cleared the table. Looking up at that face, Amber almost hesitated. But then she plunged in. "I can't drink much coffee. Could I please have milk instead?"

She was answered with a grunt as the menus slapped onto the table.

"Was that a yes?" Amber asked Wyatt quietly as the woman stomped away.

"Mavis or Maude will bring your milk." He winked. "I warned you about the service. Okay, end of an era. Micah's been a deputy here ever since he mustered out of the army. Nearly a quarter century now. He started working for the old sheriff, Nate Tate, who retired a while back, which was another end-of-an-era event around here. Anyway, at first Micah wasn't very well accepted."

"Why? Because he's Native American?"

"Bingo. A lot of those prejudices still exist. He's become kind of iconic over the years, like the old sheriff. And folks still call Gage the new sheriff, even though it's been years."

"I'm beginning to get the picture."

He nodded. "Things do change here, they just change slowly."

She was also adding together her impressions and began to feel very uncomfortable. "Wyatt? Will my staying with you cause problems? Because people are bound to talk and you're a judge…"

"God, you sound like my father," he said with a hint of exasperation. "I don't care what they say. If I did, I wouldn't have invited you."

But her stomach sank even more as she realized his father had objected to her visit. Wyatt had often struck her as the knight-errant type, willing to fight for what he thought was right, despite the consequences to himself. That could be an admirable thing at times, but sometimes not. Like possibly now.

She had to force herself to look at the menu and find something she thought she could eat. As self-absorbed as her problems had made her for the last six weeks, she hadn't lost her ability to care. She didn't want to cause this man any trouble, so she'd need to figure out something quickly.

At last she chose a grilled cheese sandwich with a side salad. Despite the lack of service, their orders were placed in front of them quickly, and Wyatt dug into what looked like a really juicy steak sandwich.

"You're rather unconventional in your approach to being a judge," she remarked. "I'm used to judges who don't take an interest beyond the law."

"I don't know that I'm unconventional. I just know these are real people with real problems, and a lot of them are my neighbors. Some come from the next county over and I may never see them again, but they're still human beings."

She looked up from her sandwich with a smile. "You were always like that. I remember how much you wanted to be a defense attorney. And why. Still tilting at windmills, I see."

He half smiled. "I don't know if they're windmills, but while there are some things justice should never see, I think she needs to take off that blindfold once in a while."

"Mercy."

"Maybe. Certainly everyone's entitled to a fair shake, and by the time some of them come in front of me, they've hardly had a fair shake in their lives."

She nodded and reached for the second half of her sandwich, glad her appetite had returned. "I worked in a different world at those big firms."

"I'm sure you did."

"Most of my clients had gotten more than their share of fair shakes in life. They were just looking for another one. Or maybe for a better-than-fair outcome." She shrugged one shoulder. "Well-heeled, successful, mostly men who thought they had the world by a string. It came as a real shock when they found out they didn't."

Distasteful, she thought. Yes, it was the way up the ladder to maybe becoming a judge herself one day, but a lot of her clients...just because they had money didn't mean she respected them.

But she did like the pro bono work she did when she could at the free legal clinic. She was going to miss that.

"Do you like chili?" Wyatt asked, drawing her out of her maunderings.

"Sure. Not the beans so much, though."

"I make it without beans. How about we have that for dinner tonight?"

"You cooking?"

He laughed. "Absolutely. The chef is going to love having an excuse."

Chapter Three

On the way home, he took a detour to the grocery. Despite having just driven all the way from Chicago, she opted to stay in the car. Instead she pulled her jacket snugly around her to wait, then decided to climb out and stroll around the parking lot.

The wind seemed to be dying a bit. To the west she saw brilliant blue sky right over the mountains, although it remained overcast overhead. The ends of the earth, she thought again, but this time with amusement. The town had some appeal to it, though, and she suspected if you lived your whole life here, you might get to know almost everyone. They wouldn't necessarily be friends, but you'd recognize them.

Having been anonymous on crowded streets for so long, she wondered how that would feel. Good? Bad? Or maybe people here were so used to it they never even thought about it.

But she thought about it now.

He didn't keep her waiting long, and as they drove back to his house, she leaned her head back and watched the passing houses. Some better kept than others, a whole mishmash of different designs, but lots of trees lining the streets. Pretty. A grace of its own.

But then they were home, and after he'd put his purchases in the refrigerator, he invited her to join him at the kitchen table.

Now, she thought edgily, he was going to want to talk. He had every right to bring up her mess. Every right to understand better. Hadn't she basically thrown herself on his mercy by coming out here, by calling him in the first place? Of course she had, and she owed him the whole sordid story. And maybe the story of everything else she'd done since starting her career. It wasn't like it was all bad.

But he surprised her with the direction he took. "What's off-limits because of the baby?"

"Off-limits?" she asked, not following.

"Foods, beverages, that kind of thing."

The question startled her a bit, because she hadn't been thinking much about that aspect. She knew to avoid alcohol and over-the-counter meds, but other than that...

He frowned faintly. "Have you seen a doctor yet, Amber?"

"Well, my regular doctor. He said to make an appointment with an obstetrician, and he gave me some vitamins to take. He also advised me to limit myself to a couple of cups of coffee but...well, I think he was expecting the obstetrician to give me all the details."

"But you haven't gone."

"Not yet." She looked down, feeling inexplicably stupid. "I'm not an idiot," she protested. "But with all that's been going on… I was going to get to it. I'm not that far along…"

"Okay." He brought her a glass of milk instead of coffee, which he made for himself. "I'm not criticizing you. You've been through a rough time. But maybe it wouldn't hurt to see the obstetrician here. Just to be on the safe side."

She didn't answer. Instead of looking at him, she turned her head and stared out through the window at the gray day. Okay, she hadn't really been dealing with the reality of this pregnancy. She'd hardly been thinking about it except in the vaguest of ways. Yes, she'd followed the directions she'd been given, but beyond that…beyond that, she didn't want to face the fact that she was becoming a mother and that her whole life and all her dreams had changed. She might tell herself she wasn't stupid, but stupidity had gotten her here, and now stupidity was keeping her from facing reality.

Too much, she thought. *Too much.* She didn't know how she was going to deal with it all. No idea where to go, how to handle it. All she knew was that she'd had to get away from that law firm. Everyone knew she'd been seeing Tom. Everyone knew he'd lied about his divorce, because he'd done it before. But so far none of them knew she'd managed to get pregnant. The one humiliation in the whole affair that hadn't become public.

But if she had stayed, it would have become very public. She suspected she wouldn't be welcome there once everyone knew about the baby. Tom was a junior partner. She was no one. Time to get out before she felt as if she were in the public stocks.

Wyatt had agreed with her once she told him what had happened. Staying at the firm would have been very uncomfortable, and while she could have lied and said the baby was someone else's…well, most people wouldn't have believed it, and she'd have had Tom trying to make her life enough of a hell that she'd quit anyway.

At least that was her read, and Wyatt had agreed that she might not be able to convince everyone that the father was someone else. How much that would affect her future at the firm was anyone's guess. Wyatt said he'd like to believe no one would give her trouble, but… He'd let that dangle.

It was her suspicion that the moment she became a potential embarrassment to Tom, her career would be in jeopardy. Maybe they'd have given her time to find another position, but she didn't want the humiliation. There was already enough of that, knowing she'd had an affair with a married man, and that others knew it as well.

She sighed and returned her attention to Wyatt. "I guess I've been trying to ignore it. To deal with the nitty-gritty of quitting my job, packing up my life and heading into the unknown. But I couldn't have stayed. I couldn't."

He nodded slowly. "You could have tried. It certainly would have been miserable, but if you said nothing, maybe they would have gotten past it."

"You said that. I wasn't buying it. If I hadn't just joined the firm last spring, maybe. But my track record was so short…" She wrapped her hands around the glass of milk and stared into the liquid. "See if I ever trust a man again."

His dark eyes turned suddenly inscrutable. "Ouch," he said quietly.

She flushed. "I don't mean you. You're different."

He merely gave her a half smile. "Of course, we all know who should be paying for this mess, but unfortunately life isn't always fair. Kicking up a fuss would probably have bought you more trouble than you'd ever want. You think this guy Tom would have retaliated in some way?"

"Probably," she said glumly. "Even if I never said a word, I'd have worried him. I'd be hanging there like a threat. I saw how he handled his cases. He's not a man you want to cross swords with if he feels threatened."

Wyatt nodded. "I accept your judgment. Never having met the guy, I have no idea what he's capable of." He paused. "Did I ever tell you about Ellie?"

She shook her head slowly, grateful for the change of subject. "Who's she?"

"I dated her for a while about a year ago. Along about the time we started to get serious, she asked me to dismiss a bunch of charges against her cousin."

Amber gasped, totally diverted from her problems. "No!"

"Oh, yes. That relationship ended instantly. So to get even, she told everyone she knows that I'm gay."

"Oh! That must have made you angry."

He grinned suddenly. "Why? I don't care. That's my business and nobody else's. Anyway, it's old news. I'm just saying, life throws curveballs. It's what we do about them that matters. I chose the high road and she tried to get even. The point is, I understand why you worried about what Tom might do. He had a job and a marriage to protect. A reputation, even. He'd probably have done everything he could to submarine you. I'm not saying he would have succeeded, but it could have made you miserable for a long time. You decided how you wanted to handle it, and here we are."

For the first time, she drank some of the milk he'd offered her. "Yes, here we are," she said after she'd dabbed her mouth with a paper napkin. "Where is that?"

He laughed. "Just take some time to figure out whatever you need to. The only thing I ask is that you get to a proper doctor. Wherever you may be in seven or eight months, you don't want to be with a baby that could have been healthier if you'd taken care of yourself."

Right now, Wyatt thought as he studied her and listened to her, the pregnancy was a major concern whether she was ready to face it or not. While he was no expert and had no personal experience, he seemed to remember hearing that the first few months could be absolutely critical to a fetus. Were vitamins and avoiding coffee enough? He had no idea.

That was the point of doctors, and he had great respect for professionals. Amber needed one, and he was determined she see one before long.

She was a beautiful woman, a very smart woman, and it troubled him to see her in this situation. From all he'd heard from her over the years, he got the feeling that she'd been one of those people for whom everything went right. No major problems, a skyrocketing career, the world on a string.

But of course, nobody got through life without their share of troubles. She'd apparently lumped many of hers into one enormous mistake. And she was devastated. Everything she'd worked for had been taken from her by a lying jackass. He had plenty of questions to ask, basic ones like, hadn't she been using protection? But it was none of his business.

His only business was to be supportive until she could figure out what she wanted to do. In the meantime, quashing his attraction to her would probably be very wise. She'd been through the wringer; she'd said she wouldn't trust men again. Having her place him in a separate category meant she didn't see him as an eligible man. Which was fine by him. Neither of them needed any complications, and she'd probably be moving on in a month or two.

Given Amber's dreams, he couldn't see her hanging around here for long.

But still, there was an errant part of him that had belonged to Amber ever since the first day they had talked. Friendship? Of course. Something more? No point in thinking about it, even though over the years he'd occasionally daydreamed about what life would have been like with her. Pointless fantasy, reawakened by phone calls and running into her at the convention. Fantasies he'd put aside again every time they rose.

She finished her milk and rose to rinse the glass at the sink. Standing there with her back to him, she began to speak. "I need to wake up," she said.

"Wake up?" Curious, he twisted in his chair to better see her, even if it was only her back.

"Wake up," she repeated. "This has been like a nightmare. Do you know how it started?"

"Which part?"

She shook her head, and a heavy sigh escaped her.

"Which part? Good question. You know working for a firm like that doesn't leave any room for a social life."

"I've heard." Not that being a judge was a whole lot better, unless he put his foot down as he had this week.

"Two thousand billable hours a year is forty hours a week for fifty weeks. Which doesn't sound all that awful until you add all the hours that aren't billable. I didn't get a day off and I didn't expect one. Not for many years to come. Your friends, such as they are, are people you work with. If you have a family, you might see them for a few minutes as you're falling into bed or running out the door in the morning. I loved most of it."

"Okay," he said to show he was listening, but unsure if she was looking for a particular response from him.

"In a few more years, if I'd been lucky and continued to rise, I'd have reached the level where I could get out of the office to go golfing with clients. I might even have been able to take an occasional weekend. The point is, though, that your whole life revolves around the firm. They even arrange the social occasions. Dinner with the partner, a party at a partner's house, where in theory you'd win some new clients. All business."

For those who wanted to get ahead in that game, he thought. Plenty of others chose an easier path, but Amber had always been driven. Law school at nineteen?

"Human nature will have its way eventually," she said. "Tom started to express interest. He was attractive, and considering we were pretty much working all the time, he was what was available. Office romances are dangerous. I knew it, but I took the chance anyway. He was in the middle of a messy divorce, he said. And I believed him."

"Why wouldn't you?"

She turned slowly to face him and folded her arms tightly. "I think that from working all the time I let parts of my development become stunted. The practice of law gave me a view of a lot of ugliness in life, but that ugliness didn't include a coworker deliberately lying to me to get me into his bed. Regardless, in the last ten years I haven't had time for a boyfriend. I only dated a couple of times, but my schedule blew everything up. So there I was, missing a massive part of life, and this coworker was suddenly pursuing me. I was flattered. I was stupid."

"You're not stupid. Some very smart people get conned, Amber."

She smiled crookedly, without humor. "Well, I got conned. Funny, it never seemed odd to me that the only time we got together was in a hotel over our lunch hour. When we had a lunch hour. It's not like I couldn't have escaped the office sometimes just for dinner. There should have been red flags all over it."

He couldn't disagree. "I imagine you really liked him."

"Of course. I thought I was falling in love. Maybe I was. But then I found out. God, that was awful. I caught one of the clerks drinking in the bathroom, and when I started to tell her she couldn't do that, she stopped me dead in my tracks. It seems I wasn't the first newbie Tom had taken advantage of, and if she hadn't been drunk she probably wouldn't have told me. Everyone kept quiet about it because they didn't want to get fired."

She shook her head, then held out one arm, almost a pleading gesture. "I broke it off immediately, of course. He started giving me a hard time, but there wasn't a whole lot he could do except make me uncomfortable. I was uncomfortable enough that all my coworkers probably knew what had been happening. I felt so humiliated!"

"I'm sure your coworkers knew you had been used," he offered quietly.

"I'm sure. At least that's what I kept telling myself. Until I found out I was pregnant." A bitter laugh escaped her. "Birth control fails sometimes. I was one of the minuscule percentage of failures. Ironic, huh?"

"I think it stinks. I don't find it ironic at all." He wished he could hug her, but he wasn't sure that would help. If she needed to talk, the best thing he could do was listen.

"Anyway, that's when I called you. I could stick out the knowing looks. I figured the whispers would go away. But a pregnancy? Everyone would know. And I have no doubt Tom would have used every bit of influence he had to get rid of me if he knew, because he could deny everything except a paternity test."

As a lawyer and then a judge, Wyatt had learned to separate his emotions from his thinking. He had to. He was the one who had to remain objective as much as possible. He'd be no good to a client if feelings clouded his judgment, and that hadn't changed much on the bench. He might dispense mercy when he could, but he still had to have an unemotional, clear grasp of the situation, the facts and the law.

He was finding that objectivity very difficult to achieve right now. In fact, damn near impossible. He looked at the young woman, his friend, nearly curled up on herself as she relived her nightmare, and he would have dearly loved to get his hands on this guy Tom. His fists had clenched, and he had to make an effort to relax them. He didn't want to frighten Amber with the impulse to violence that was building in him now.

"Anyway," she said presently, "it's been a nightmare, especially since I found out I was pregnant. I couldn't believe that on top of everything else. Maybe I still can't believe it. It's almost like if I close my eyes and pull the blankets over my head, the bad things will go away." She shook her head. "I know better than that. And you're right, whether I'm ready to accept it or not, I need to take care of the child growing inside me. That's one thing I can still do right."

His chest felt as if a steel band wrapped around it, and it tightened at those words. One thing she could do right?

"Amber…" Maybe he was wrong, but he remembered the woman he used to know. Had she entirely given up because of this? He wouldn't have expected it.

Maybe she just needed time and space to get used to so much. It sure as hell had been a huge, shocking change.

It had been a month since she first phoned him. Back then the emotionless delivery he'd heard from her had been understandable. He'd believed she'd been merely discussing her options, ways to deal with an untenable situation. But now she seemed to be in some kind of shock. Maybe she had been when she first called, and her clinical attitude had been some kind of an emotional withdrawal. Did this mean it was now becoming emotionally real to her?

He'd thought he'd been offering refuge to a friend, a safe place where she could rest and decide what to do. Now he was wondering just exactly what she needed, and if he could even begin to help her deal with what was clearly a bigger trauma than he'd imagined.

A friend quitting her job because a relationship failed and she was pregnant hadn't sounded so bad. Now that he was getting the dimensions of all this, he didn't think *nightmare* was too strong a description.

"Anyway," she said after a minute or so, "sorry for the dump."

"Don't be sorry. You needed to dump on someone. And maybe your friends weren't listening."

"Friends?" She shook her head and at last returned to sit at the table with him. "I had coworkers, colleagues. People I knew, but no one I was able to get intimate with. I was always on guard. You have to be careful what you tell a coworker."

There was no arguing that. He went to pour himself some fresh coffee, asking her if she wanted anything.

"I'm full from lunch. Thanks."

When he faced her across the table again, he was still trying to find something to say to her. She'd been unsparingly honest with him, telling him far more than she had on the phone, and in the process giving him a better view of the dimensions of all she faced. Come here for a few weeks to catch her breath and make a plan?

That's what he'd thought, but now he wasn't so sure it was going to work that easily. She was still having trouble believing she was pregnant. Maybe she still hadn't really started to believe any of this.

If so, it would take more than a few weeks.

"Wyatt? Remember when we first met in law school? We were in the first week and I was already overwhelmed."

"I remember." He'd never forget it. He'd seen not only a pretty young woman, but someone who didn't look old enough to be facing the fire of law school. He'd thought he'd detected a bit of panic in her gaze, so he'd wandered over to the bench where she was sitting beside a pile of books, handouts and notebooks, and introduced himself.

"L-1 is a hard year," he'd offered. "I'm in my last year."

Her head had swiveled then, and she'd truly seen him. "I'm scared to death."

From that moment, they'd become friends. "I remember," he said again.

"You seemed so calm," she said. "And friendly. You told me things to pay attention to…oh, you gave me a load of good advice for doing well and getting through it. But I never told you something."

He waited the way he waited in a courtroom, knowing that important information was coming his way.

"I didn't want to be there," she said. "And I don't just mean the first weeks, or the overwhelmed feeling. I didn't want to be in law school at all."

That shocked him. He'd never imagined that law school hadn't been her choice. He'd spent three years surrounded by people who wanted to be no place else. "Then why did you apply?"

"Because of my parents. I didn't graduate early be-

cause I wanted to. I didn't go to college at sixteen because I wanted to. And I sure as hell didn't go to law
school because I wanted to. Although I have to admit,
I started to like the law. I still enjoy the practice of it.
Parts of it, anyway."

But he saw her in an entirely different way now. So
much suddenly became clear: her push for success,
her moving up the ladder in firms that could tear the
soul out of a person simply through overwork, client
demands and the constant threat of losing your job if
an important client grew unhappy. And he also understood something else. "So your parents don't know
anything about this…situation?"

"Not a thing. Mom passed away five years ago,
but no, my father doesn't know. I guess he's going to
have to know eventually, but not right now. He'll be
furious."

Wyatt would have liked to argue with her, but how
could he? He'd never met Amber's father.

She sighed and reached for the napkin she had used
to wipe her mouth and smoothed it out with her fingers. "I've been a wuss," she said finally.

"That's one thing I'd never call you."

She lifted her head with a smile that didn't reach her
eyes. "I let myself be used to fulfill their dreams for
me. It only got worse when Dad told me after Mom's
funeral that she'd be so proud of all I'd accomplished."

"More pressure."

"Exactly. Evidently somewhere along the way I
failed to grow a spine."

He doubted that was a fair assessment, but he could
understand where it came from. "Well," he said finally,
"you're here now, you can stay as long as you like and

the only thing I'm going to pressure you about is seeing a doctor."

She nodded. "Fair enough." After a moment she asked tentatively, "Did you feel pressured because your dad was a lawyer?"

"He didn't pressure me," Wyatt said truthfully. "Yeah, we talked about me going into the practice with him, but he didn't offer a single objection when I took two years after I finished my undergrad degree to see if I liked something else."

She shook her head a little. "I can't imagine it."

"Evidently not. It sounds to me like you never had a chance to take a deep breath."

She closed her eyes briefly but didn't answer. "I guess you're saving my life again."

Two things struck him in that. Offering her a place to stay was hardly saving her life. Over-the-top. But then… "Again? What do you mean?"

"You saved me that first year in law school. I was totally at sea, totally unprepared to be so much on my own. For the first time in my life, my parents weren't watching my every move and helping me make every decision. I could have made some really big mistakes. But you were always there to remind me."

"In short," he said almost irritably, "I was another parent."

"No!" That caused her eyes to widen. "No, that isn't what I meant. I didn't want to fail. I dreaded failing. I needed every bit of help you gave me. That's all I meant."

He wasn't sure he was buying it. He had thought they were friends, that he was simply helping another student when she ran into trouble with her studies. The idea that he might have been in loco parentis for her didn't sit well at all with him. He'd helped her with law issues. The most advice he'd given her apart from that was to never let herself fall behind. He'd hashed out legal arguments with her. But never, not once, could he remember giving her advice on how to live her life. Hell, he hadn't even paid attention to who she was dating, if she dated anyone.

"I guess I said that wrong," she offered. "I didn't mean it the way you took it. I liked you as a friend. I admired a lot of things about you. I tried to be a little like you. But I never saw you as a parent figure. Ever."

He hoped she wasn't lying, because here they were in his house, her pregnant and unemployed, and if she was looking for a father figure, he wasn't prepared to apply for the role. No way.

Finally he spoke again, seeking different ground. "In the midst of all this upset, have you had any chance at all to think about what you want to do next? I realize you're probably still feeling sideswiped, but you must have had some impulses."

"I have. But can I trust them when I'm so emotionally messed up? I've pretty much concluded I'm done with silk-stocking law firms, though. Even if gossip doesn't get around, I'm not sure that I want to keep living that way. And then there's this baby. Much as I seem to be in denial, it keeps popping into my head. How could I continue a job like that with a child? Turn it over to someone else to raise?" Her mouth drew down at the corners. "I don't think I can do that, Wyatt."

That statement eased some of the tension inside him. Why, he couldn't say. Her life, her baby, her decision, but somehow he felt better about her knowing that she wasn't going to dump the child on a full-time nanny.

"A lot of people might put it up for adoption," he said, hating the words even as he spoke them. But it was his place to be logical, not emotional. Life had drilled that into him.

"No," she said without hesitation. "I can't do that. There's like... I don't know exactly how to explain it. But there was a moment, absolutely etched into my mind and heart, when I knew there wasn't going to be an abortion and there wasn't going to be an adoption. Everything in me clamped into a tight ball of resistance as soon as I thought of those things."

He nodded and released a breath he hadn't known he'd been holding. Why her decision should matter so much to him, he couldn't begin to guess. "Then it appears you have a whole new life to build."

"To put it mildly," she agreed. Placing her chin in her hand, she smiled at him. "It's been awful, Wyatt. Just awful. Everything blowing up around me, finding out I'd been lied to and used by someone I trusted, leaving my new job...it's been terrible. But I feel the most ridiculous sense of freedom for the first time in my life."

He nodded in understanding, but wondered how much of that was real and how much was a reaction to all the stress. He hoped it was real, because she sure as hell had blown up her bridges behind her.

Chapter Four

The room Wyatt had given her was lovely, Amber thought. She hadn't really seen much last night because she'd been so tired, but when she came upstairs to change into more comfortable clothes for the afternoon and evening, and maybe to grab a short nap, she took it all in.

A wide four-poster bed with its head against a wall covered in floral wallpaper. A rocking chair with comfortable pillows, a small writing desk, an armoire that looked like it was as old as the house and a surprisingly large walk-in closet.

A person could almost live in a room like this. Heavy rugs were scattered across the wood floor, their pastel colors matching the roses on the wall. It felt fresh and new, yet it retained the charm of an older age. When was the last time she'd seen wallpaper like that?

She changed into jeans. Her pregnancy hadn't yet started expanding her middle, or at least not enough to affect what she wore. Over that, she pulled an off-white cotton sweater. Autumn was here and there was a slight chill in the house, but she couldn't stand wool. She had occasionally thought with amusement that a lawyer without a wool suit was doomed to failure. So far she'd managed, though. There were enough cotton blends that she'd been able to look properly well-to-do. Once she'd found a tailor who got it, anyway.

She still felt tired from all the traveling, packing and stress, but lying down only sent her mind roaming anxious pathways. No good. Finally she rose, put on some ballet slippers and returned downstairs. She found Wyatt in the kitchen, doing something with beef in a frying pan that smelled absolutely delicious.

"Hi," she said.

He glanced over his shoulder and smiled. "No nap?"

"Couldn't quiet my mind. Is that for chili?"

"Yup. There must be a million recipes for it. I've tried a lot of them."

She managed a small laugh. "Fond of it, are you?"

"My fondness for chili is so famous that I've been asked to judge the chili cook-off the last few years."

"Seriously?"

"Seriously. Grab a seat. If you want a cold drink there's a choice in the fridge. If you want hot, I can make some more cocoa."

She chose a soft drink and passed close to the stove to see what looked like cubes of high-quality meat browning, already aromatic with seasonings. "I always use hamburger."

"Hamburger and beans. You can do a lot with those."

"So how did your chili become famous?"

He laughed as she sat at the table. "My chili isn't famous. My love of it is. When I have friends over, it's chili. When I throw a bigger bash, it's a bigger pot of chili. When I'm invited to a backyard barbecue, I bring some chili. Not always the same recipe, but it's a great way to feed a crowd easily. And I *do* enjoy it."

"So no fancy canapés?"

"No. Just hearty, stomach-filling food." He chuckled quietly and pulled the frying pan off the burner. "How hot and spicy do you prefer? I don't want to burn a hole in your tongue or stomach."

"Medium."

"Good enough." He went back to adding ingredients to the pan—tomato sauce, some floury substance he said was masa and more seasonings. Then he put the chili on to simmer and joined her at the table.

"So, too anxious to nap?"

"That'll wear off," she said. "I guess I need to just settle things inside me. Get used to it. And you couldn't possibly want to hear me talk endlessly about myself, Wyatt." She shook her head a little. "I've got one topic and one topic only lately. As for everything before… well, most of that wasn't very interesting, either."

She watched him smile and remembered how much she had always liked his smile. Something about it seemed to radiate warmth and charm. "I think you're very interesting," he answered. "But…what else would you like to talk about?"

An answering smile was born on her own face. Despite everything, he could make her smile. After the last month, she appreciated what a wonder that was.

All her smiles had been forced, required, and none of them had been real. Until she saw Wyatt again.

"Well," she began, "how did you become a judge?"

He gave a bark of laughter. "Not even an interesting story. For some reason known only to them, some members of the Wyoming bar gave my name to the judicial commission and I was selected. Now I'm up for a retention vote in November."

Amber felt her heart lurch. "Wyatt…that's only a few weeks away. Me staying with you, could it cause you problems?"

He shrugged one shoulder. "Fact is, Amber, I don't care. I like being a judge just fine. I also liked practicing law with my dad. If folks around here don't want me on the bench, well, it's not as if I'd be out of work. Hell, I can't even campaign, so they either like what I've been doing or not."

She shook her head a little. "Most of them probably have no idea what you've been doing on the bench. But gossip about you having a woman staying with you, that could get around, couldn't it?"

"Maybe it already has. Gossip around here has wings."

Her stomach sank for a whole new reason. "You never should have invited me here. I'll never forgive myself if you aren't retained."

"You probably would be the least of it. As I was telling my dad the other day, this *is* the twenty-first century."

Amber's head snapped up, and her heart pounded uncomfortably. "So he thought it was a bad idea, too?"

"It was more a case of the pot calling the kettle black. He has a thirty-year history of sharing his home with a variety of women, but he still gets clients. Nothing to worry about."

"I hope not." But now she felt a little sick. "Maybe I could move to a hotel."

"I wouldn't put my worst enemy in that fleabag. No, you're staying here, and I don't want you to worry about it. If people choose to boot me because I have a friend visiting…well, let 'em."

Of all the things she had considered when she decided to accept his invitation to stay here, she had never once thought that she might be putting him in an untenable position as a judge. So very selfish of her not to have given that a thought.

In fact, now that she faced it, she realized she had pretty much become a selfish person all the way around. When was the last time she'd seriously given consideration to anyone's needs but her own? So totally focused on her career…had she ever really thought about anyone else?

Mad that Tom had betrayed her, yes, but as she was busy considering what that meant to her, had she given a single thought to Tom's wife? Of course not. When Wyatt had told her she was welcome to stay with him while she figured things out, had she ever once asked if it might cause him any problems?

Of course not. Filled with self-disgust, she pushed back from the table and ran up the stairs to her room.

For the first time it struck her that not only had her parents constantly pushed her, but they had raised her to believe she was the only one who mattered. Everything was about Amber.

No wonder she'd hardly given a thought to the baby inside her. Pure selfishness.

* * *

Wyatt guessed he shouldn't have mentioned the upcoming retention vote. He certainly hadn't expected her response to it, or that the first thing she would consider was that her mere presence in his home might cost him the election.

Amber was turning into more of a puzzle than he'd anticipated. But then, he'd only really known her well when she was nineteen. A whole lot of years lay between then and now, and life changed people.

She surely couldn't believe that she and she alone could make people vote not to retain him. He didn't think there were that many uptight, judgmental people in this county. Everyone had their peccadilloes, and as he'd discovered as a judge, some of them had major ones. Who was staying with whom seemed the least of it.

No, if he wasn't retained it would be for other reasons, but the likelihood of that happening was slim to none. Generally speaking, it would take a truly major scandal to get him thrown off the bench, the kind of scandal that would make headlines outside this county.

Anything could happen, of course. Regardless of what Earl thought about Amber staying here, Earl himself could be a major liability in the upcoming election. Thirty years of affairs, and who could guess how many clients he might have angered over the decades. That would have far more of an impact than Amber's presence.

Although he was sure Earl would view it very differently.

He sighed, wishing he hadn't mentioned the election, although she'd probably have heard about it one way or another. He was planning to introduce her to people in the hopes she wouldn't have to spend too much time alone when he was working. One of them would have mentioned it, even if he hadn't.

But there was absolutely no reason for her to take blame for the outcome.

She had changed, he thought. The years had changed her. Well, they'd probably changed him, too, but it remained there was little of the girl he'd known left, and yet perhaps too much of that nineteen-year-old.

Or maybe she was overreacting because of her pregnancy. How would he know? It was easy to assume that such a massive physical change would have emotional effects, but that skated too close to the edge of sexism for him to be comfortable with the thought.

Just leave it, he told himself. She'd been through so much she was a bit rocky. Give her a few days of stability, and she might begin to feel better.

He really felt for her. No question that she'd been through a lot, more than most people would handle well. He needed to give her space to deal with the emotional toll. She'd been sailing along fairly well and then this.

It would be a test of her spirit, all right.

But then, he thought about what she'd said about her parents pushing her. Had she ever had time to figure out what *she* wanted from life? Apparently now she was going to get it, wanted or not.

Because Amber was right: except for her baby, she was utterly free for the first time in her life. No parental pressure and a whopping big mess to push away any internal drive she'd been feeling to reach the heights.

A crash for sure. But if that drive had all been the

result of the way she'd been raised, she was sure going to be at sea now.

Everything she had been taught to consider important had just blown up on her. Transitioning would involve a lot more than just finding a new job. It was going to involve a whole new way of thinking about herself and her future.

He was glad he wasn't facing that. He'd sprung out on his own for a couple of years after college, tested his wings, decided what he wanted was to be here. He'd been his own decision maker.

Aside from leaving a job and keeping a baby, had Amber ever decided anything for herself?

This mess appeared to be growing bigger by the moment.

Amber cried for the first time since everything had blown up on her. She seldom cried, mostly because her parents had taught her that tears were useless and that instead of indulging in them, she ought to be fixing the problem.

But she cried now, and she didn't give a darn whether it was a waste of energy, or that it was useless. She needed to cry more than she ever had in her life. Everything was a mess, and she seemed to be creating a new mess just by coming here and...

Her self-image had blown up. Like getting slapped in the head by a two-by-four, her entire view had just shifted so much that she felt like a stranger in her own skin.

Selfish. She had never thought of herself that way before, but as she tested the word, the truth of it settled harshly in her heart. Oh, she donated her time and money to charity, she never passed a homeless person without giving them something and she thought about the ills of the world and bemoaned them. But when it came to Amber, only Amber mattered.

At an early age her parents had set her feet on a path and hadn't let her divert from it. They had told her she would do great things for the world and she had believed them. But their idea of doing great things had meant climbing to the top rung of financial and career success.

Was that really so great? She'd watched Wyatt in his courtroom that morning and had been touched. He'd been unsparing when people deserved it, but what had reached her most was how often he tried to help one of the miscreants get things sorted out. It hadn't just been the man who couldn't read. There had been others, like the woman who had no auto insurance because she couldn't afford it. He'd talked to her about her situation in depth and had suspended sentence, giving her two weeks and a reference to a charity that would help her get the insurance. If she came to the clerk of the court with an insurance card, the charge would be dropped.

How many judges would bother with that? Of course, when she was in court she was trying very different cases. Cases that involved money, mostly civil litigation between parties in contract disputes. Those people were able to hire the best law firms and really didn't need the kind of mercy Wyatt got to show in his courtroom.

So maybe there were plenty of judges like him. How would she know? But the difference was striking, and she suspected that had had something to do with this abrupt internal shift.

Wyatt was a good judge. Why had she never once thought of him and the problems she might cause him? That question hung in her mind while her tears dried.

She hadn't thought of him. She hadn't thought much about her baby. She certainly hadn't spared a thought for the wife of the man who had betrayed her.

No, it was all about Amber's humiliation, Amber's pain, Amber's feeling that she had been stupid. Amber's messed-up life.

And the desire to get away from her humiliation had led her here. To an old friend she could perhaps now add to her list of mistakes. She'd never forgive herself if he lost this election. Retention elections were rarely lost unless something happened to make an awful lot of people think you weren't fit to be a judge.

In a big city her presence here wouldn't even be discussed. But this was a small town, and she had some experience of small towns. Her parents had left one when she was young because her father had been accused of having an affair with an important man's wife. He claimed he hadn't, and she didn't know what the truth was, but life in the little town had become untenable for them.

Sure, this was the twenty-first century. But how much had attitudes really changed about some behaviors?

Then there was the baby. *Her* baby. Wyatt had expressed more concern about it than she had yet. She hadn't gone to the doctor for prenatal care, she'd gone to have her pregnancy confirmed. So far, she hadn't followed the most important order of all: get to an obstetrician.

So what did that say about her? Was she wishing the child away? Unable to cope with what it would mean to her future? Hoping something went awry if she just ignored it long enough?

A fresh wave of tears hit her, and she buried her face in a damp pillow so the sounds couldn't escape the room.

It would be very easy to hate herself.

She just hoped Wyatt didn't come to hate her, too.

Wyatt finished making the chili and wondered if he should heat the tortillas now or wait for her. Or if he should go up and see if she was all right.

He wasn't sure what he had expected from Amber's visit, but matters were taking some unexpected turns. He hadn't been prepared for what appeared to have the makings of an epic self-reevaluation on her part.

Yet why should that be surprising, in light of all that had happened to her? Maybe she'd been running on automatic until she got here. That wouldn't be surprising, either, especially given what she'd said about her parents.

So they had pushed her all the way. Early college, then law school at too young an age. Had Amber ever had a real chance to find *herself*? He knew how those large law firms worked. They pretty much owned you. If life had been all work and no play, how could she ever find Amber?

And if that's what she was doing right now, maybe he ought to prepare himself for some major fireworks, because it wasn't going to be easy. Whoever she thought she was had just been blown up. As always, he wished he could help, but he had absolutely no idea what kind of help he might be able to offer. Just that he still had a place in his heart for her after all these years, so he gave a damn about her. That wasn't likely to fix much.

Sighing, he gave the chili one more stir, deciding that the spices must have blended well enough by now and the pepper had grown as hot as it would. Then he heard light steps approaching, solving one of his problems: he wouldn't have to go disturb her in her room.

She smiled as he turned, but he could see her eyes were swollen. She'd been crying. Oh, hell. "You okay?" he asked immediately.

"Fine. A little self-knowledge can be overwhelming. I've never had this much time to just think about myself and my life. Difficult but informative."

"I hope you're not thinking bad things," he said carefully.

"I'm thinking there's a lot I don't like about myself. Man, that chili smells wonderful!"

He accepted the change of subject and got the dishes out, deciding that eating in the kitchen would be cozier than that mausoleum of a dining room. Some of his forebears had had grandiose notions of themselves.

Amber immediately started helping, placing the bowls, spoons and napkins so that they would sit across from each other.

"To drink?" she asked.

He usually enjoyed a beer with this meal, but out of deference to her pregnant state, he opted for water. She found glasses and filled them with water.

"Do you want tortillas with this?" he asked. "I can heat them in a jiffy. Or we can just have crackers."

"Crackers, please," she answered.

He pulled out the box of soda crackers and placed it on the table. "Be careful of my mother's silver serving box. It's been in the family for generations."

To his relief, she laughed. "You mentioned your father but not your mother."

"Ah." He ladled chili into each bowl, then put the pan back on the stove. "My mother died when I was almost eight. She slipped and fell on the ice and cracked the back of her head pretty badly."

"I am so sorry!"

"Me, too. But that was thirty years ago, and while I still miss her at times, I'm used to it." They sat facing each other. "Are you going to call home, Amber? Your father will wonder where you've gone if you haven't told him."

"He's used to me not calling for long periods because of work. I'll get around to it. Not that I want to hear what he has to say."

He hesitated, a spoonful of chili on the way to his mouth, watching her pull out a few crackers and place them in her bowl. "You're thirty. Why would you be worried about what they might say?"

Stupid question, and he knew it. Earl was always kibitzing about Wyatt's life. But it bothered him that she didn't want to tell her father. He'd have thought a woman in her situation would want to talk to family. Instead she had chosen him.

When it came to issues like this, he was about as inexperienced as it was possible to be. Looking firmly down at his bowl, he began to eat.

Amber was quiet for a while, except to tell him how delicious the chili was. Then she asked, "So you have a variety of recipes?"

"I collect them. Some are better than others, of course, but I find it a whole lot easier to entertain a group of people with a meal like this."

"Do you entertain often?"

"I have friends. Some will be coming over Saturday night. Then there are the others."

"Others?"

He winked at her. "Yeah, the people I have to be polite to because of my job. County commissioners, city councilmen, a couple of local magistrates who help handle my caseload, other important people."

"You don't like them?" She didn't seem shocked by the idea.

"It's not that I don't like them. They're just not my closest friends. I have more friends in the sheriff's department, for some reason. Then there's a couple of schoolteachers, some ranchers, oh, a whole assortment. You'll get to meet some of them."

He couldn't interpret her reaction. Her face revealed nothing, but finally she said, "That'll be nice."

"It's not a work thing," he said, then regretted the tone of his voice. He didn't want to add any more discomfort to her plate. "You don't have to come if you don't want to."

"I'll come," she said quietly. "It'd probably be good for people to learn who I am. Just an old friend visiting."

What was going on here? He had begun to think they were getting past the awkwardness, then she had run upstairs for a couple of hours and come back with swollen eyes, which meant she must have been crying. Why couldn't she share that with him? Why go hide away when she might most need some kind of understanding and comfort?

He didn't think he was particularly special, but he *could* listen. He'd expected to do a lot of it when she arrived here. He had figured she'd want to rant about how everything had gone to hell, maybe cry a bit, maybe start thinking about options and talking about them.

Instead… It struck him as odd, but he didn't remember her being so remote when they were in law school. But maybe he just didn't remember correctly. He wondered what had built those cold walls around her. What had made her feel she needed to hide herself.

Hell, he was mostly an open book. Of course, he lived in a town where he could hardly have been anything else. But what had shut Amber down like this?

He made up his mind then and there that he was going to find out.

She helped him clean up after dinner, then he announced he had some work to do.

"Decisions from last week," he said. "I picked them up this morning, so I need to read them over then sign them. You can come into my office with me down the hall if you want, or I can show you the entertainment room."

She blinked. She'd dealt with a lot of rich muckety-mucks in her career, but she would never have expected Wyatt to be in the class who could afford that. "You have an entertainment room?"

He laughed. "A spare room. I kinda rattle around

in here by myself, if you haven't noticed. So I just put the TV, DVDs and sound system in there and left the living room for when I have people over. And…you'll find a lot of books in there, too. We've always been a family for buying books."

She eyed him, feeling inexplicably amused. "No e-reader?"

"Of course I have one. I even have both a computer and a tablet for working on. Modern in every way."

His wink drew a laugh from her. He made her feel good, she realized. But he always had, she thought, looking back over the years. Even in law school when she'd been so overwhelmed, he'd had a way of getting her to relax and keep things in proportion. She could definitely use some proportion now.

But gazing at him, she also found her mind wandering a different path. How could she ever have been attracted to Tom? Because he flattered her? Because he was the only guy around that she could manage to have a relationship with, and the only one willing to risk the difficulties of a romantic relationship with a colleague?

Because he was her only choice?

But so soon after some of the biggest shocks and disappointment of her life, she was feeling a strong attraction to Wyatt. Was she crazy? A stupid question to ask herself when she thought back to their law school days and the huge, secret crush she had had on him. Wyatt was the only guy in school she'd wanted to date, and as a result she didn't date at all.

He was an attractive man with a fine physique of broad shoulders and narrow hips. His face was strong, almost patrician, but one of the things she liked most was the way the corners of his eyes crinkled when he smiled. Everything about him physically would draw the female eye, but nothing about his behavior invited it. She wondered if it was Ellie, his past interest, who had caused him to put up the off-limits signs she sensed, or if they'd always been there. Or if it was just her. He'd definitely been off-limits to her back in law school.

It did seem odd that he hadn't been snatched up at his age, though. She doubted this place was crawling with so many eligible bachelors that he would have been overlooked. Yet here he was, unattached.

And gorgeous.

She looked down, hoping she hadn't revealed her sexual response to him. Now *that* could make things very uncomfortable for them both. He'd offered her a place out of the storm to collect herself. That wouldn't last long if she made him feel uncomfortable in his own house.

So she opted for the entertainment room and some reality TV show that she hardly saw. She was sure that if she'd followed him to his office, she would have sat staring at him like a starstruck kid.

Because for the first time since law school, Amber looked past the end of her own nose and saw once again the man she had wanted years ago. Attraction had slipped past the edges of the nightmare and awakened her to never-fulfilled possibilities.

Possibilities that weren't for her. And certainly not when she was pregnant with another man's child.

Chapter Five

Amber awoke in the morning to realize she'd slept all night in front of the TV. Some morning show was on, murmuring quietly, but she wasn't interested.

Sitting up slowly, she felt a little stiff, even though the recliner had been comfortable. Not moving at all while she slept wasn't a good thing. Events and the long trip must have taken more out of her than she realized.

The clock on the box beneath the TV told her it was past nine. She must have slept close to twelve hours.

The minute she stood up, however, she felt sick, so sick that she ran for the hall bath and had dry heaves for a few minutes. Sweating and shaking, she sat on the bathroom floor and waited for the nausea to pass.

It didn't pass, but it settled a bit. Morning sickness? She couldn't remember what her doctor had said about it if anything, but she had the impression it should have started earlier. Or maybe not. She was still in her first trimester. Wyatt was right, she had to get to an obstetrician, because suddenly she was staring straight at the reality of her condition and accepting the fact that she didn't know a damn thing about it. Not one thing.

If she'd needed another wakeup call, she'd just gotten it.

Eventually, she dared to stand, waiting a couple of minutes to be sure things had settled a bit. She finally took a shower and changed into fresh clothes, all the while wondering if the nausea would ever quit.

Downstairs she found a note from Wyatt in the kitchen.

I'll be in court for a trial, don't know exactly when I'll be done. The fridge and cupboards are full, so help yourself to anything. P.S. Asked a friend to stop by and look in on you.

Oh, great. She didn't know if she was ready for that, especially the way she felt now.

Eating seemed impossible. Searching the refrigerator, she found some apple juice that looked possible. She poured a small glass and tested herself with a single sip. It stayed down.

Obstetrician, she reminded herself, except she didn't see a phone book anywhere. Of course not. Who used phone books anymore?

After she finished about four ounces of apple juice, she decided to go look for Wyatt's office. He had a computer in there, and maybe even that old-fashioned notion called a phone book. She had her laptop in her car, but she'd have no idea where or how to hook it up here.

Pulling her cardigan closer about her, she noticed for the first time that some sun was showing outside and leaves were no longer whirling around. Inside, however, she felt chilly. She wondered if it was warmer out there.

She also knew the weather was the last thing that should be preoccupying her. There were serious matters on her plate, and she was evading them.

Six weeks ago, she'd learned the truth about Tom. Two weeks after that she'd taken a home pregnancy test and found out the worst. A month ago, after talking to Wyatt, she'd given her notice at the firm, accepted a generous severance package even though she didn't deserve it—she was pretty sure she knew why it had been offered, however—and the firm had sent her on her way without letting her finish out her notice. They apparently wanted her gone as much as she wanted to be gone.

All very civilized, but a whole lot of butt covering for everyone, including her. Bad enough she'd had an affair with a married junior partner. How much worse if they'd learned of the pregnancy.

So she'd skedaddled, packed up, escaped her lease and headed straight for one of the only people on earth she felt she could trust.

And during all this, she'd been nursing some painful emotional wounds, trying to adjust to a different self-image and failing, and not considering what she was going to do next.

She'd been overwhelmed again, like the first week of law school. And once again there was Wyatt. She hoped he didn't feel used, because she feared that was exactly what she was doing.

Before she could look for Wyatt's office, the doorbell rang and she froze. This must be the friend he'd sent. A wave of rebellion rose in her and she considered not answering. Then she felt like an idiot for not wanting to.

"Stop dithering," she said aloud. This wasn't like her.

Marching to the front door, she opened it and found a lovely woman standing there. "Hi," the woman said, tossing her blond hair back from her face. "I'm Hope Cashford, a friend of Wyatt's. He asked me to stop by and look in on you when I dropped my daughter off at preschool."

Amber blinked, surprised. When Wyatt had written *friend* on his note, she'd expected a guy. Or an older woman. Certainly not a beauty.

"Hi, I'm Amber Towers. Would you like to come in?"

"Love to," Hope said.

Amber didn't quite know whether to take her to the living room or kitchen, but shouldn't she make coffee or something?

"It's hard being a new guest in someone else's house," Hope said. She slipped her arm through Amber's and led the way straight to the kitchen. "I'll make coffee even though I guess you don't want any. Do you mind?"

"How could I mind and why wouldn't I want any?"

Hope paused midstep to look at her. "Morning sickness?" she asked gently.

Amber gasped. "Does it show?"

"No," Hope said cheerfully. "Wyatt told me you're

pregnant. And trust me, I have a similar story, so we've got a lot to talk about."

Astonished, all Amber could do was sit at the table while Hope made coffee as if she knew her way around the kitchen. "How are we similar?" she asked.

"To the extent that we were both done wrong by men and got pregnant, I think we've got something in common."

"Maybe," Amber agreed, waiting to hear more. This was so frank that it surprised her. This woman didn't know her at all.

Hope came to the table as the coffee started brewing, reached into her jacket pocket and took out a business card. "This is a great obstetrical practice. I use them, and now there's a woman doctor there as well, if that matters to you. I was further along when Cash took me in, but this guy didn't even scold me. His new partner seems every bit as nice. Anyway, you keep that card."

Amber put her fingers on it and smiled weakly. "I was just thinking about this before you arrived. Thank you."

"Wyatt said you needed a doc. So..." She grinned and pulled a mug out of the cupboard. "You can have a cup if you haven't already, or should I make you something else?"

"My stomach's upset. Thank you, but I don't feel like eating or drinking anything right now."

"Ah, so it *is* the dreaded morning sickness. Have you met the soda cracker?"

"Cracker?"

Hope grinned and slipped her jacket off, hanging

it over the back of a chair. "Let me get you a few. Try them slowly. They might settle your tummy."

Soon Hope had placed a half dozen crackers on a plate in front of her, along with a glass of water. "I kept the dang things beside my bed the first three months. I couldn't even get up until I'd eaten a few. You don't seem as bad."

Amber had to smile back. "If you don't count my time in the bathroom this morning."

"Then you definitely need to see the doc soon. Anyway." She finally sat with her mug of coffee, still smiling at Amber. "You may not want to tell me much about what happened to you, but I'll gladly share my story. It kind of made the rounds thanks to my husband's teenage daughter. Not that I'm surprised. I was raised in Dallas and there were few secrets in my circle there, I can tell you."

Amber nibbled a cracker slowly, feeling her curiosity growing. "How'd you get here?"

"I went on the run." Hope's face shadowed. "My fiancé, who had been tapped to become a candidate for the US Senate, raped me."

Amber gasped, feeling her heart squeeze. "Oh, my God."

Hope shrugged. "I'm over it, thanks to Cash. But long story short, my family had a lot of money, my fiancé Scott was the perfect choice for them, I was apparently the perfect choice to be his wife and none of them were going to let a little rape and a pregnancy get in the way. I was a prisoner in my own home with two choices—have an abortion or marry Scott quickly. You can imagine how I felt about that. So I ran as soon as I had the opportunity. I wound up here with only a hundred dollars left to my name, and Cash hired me to be a nanny to his daughter." She smiled. "I am so glad about how it all turned out."

"And Wyatt became your friend?" Certainly a good enough friend that Wyatt had felt free to tell her about Amber and her pregnancy, and her need for a doctor.

"Yeah, actually. Cash has known him most of his life, and when we decided I should adopt Cash's daughter, Wyatt helped. But I had the chance to meet him before then. He's a nice man. He mentioned that you became friends in law school?"

Amber nodded and nibbled another cracker. It was staying down, and the nausea eased a bit. She hoped it kept easing. "I was in my first year, he was in his last, and he was a great help. I'm not sure I would have survived without his advice."

Hope laughed quietly. "I can imagine that man being a great help, but don't put yourself down. You'd probably have made it, even if it was harder. So…what happened to you?"

Amber hesitated. Hope hadn't given her many details, so she supposed she could skim over the most humiliating stuff and just give an outline. "Bad office romance. I had to leave and he doesn't know I'm pregnant."

Hope held her mug to her face with both hands and regarded Amber over it. "Did he lie to you?"

"Hell, yes. I didn't know he was married." And it felt so surprisingly good to just say it. There it was, the ugly thing, out there in plain view. She hadn't been reluctant to tell Wyatt, but she had no desire to tell anyone else—yet she just had.

"What a creep," Hope remarked. "And don't worry,

I won't tell anyone. Certainly not my mouthy eldest daughter, who spread my own story far and wide. But how awful for you!"

"Not as bad as a rape," Amber said weakly, fighting the all-too-familiar urge to just slip into a hole and pull the ground in over her. Her chest had begun to tighten again, making it harder to breathe. But it had felt good to say it. Why did she want to run from it again?

"Oh, I don't know," Hope said. "You were violated in a different way. Used. I know what that feels like. You come away feeling dirty and humiliated even when it wasn't your own fault."

Amber lifted her gaze, the hard knot that had been growing in her chest easing some. "That's true," she admitted. This woman *did* understand, and she wasn't judging Amber. She drew a long, shaky breath.

"It gets better," Hope said gently. "What's more, there's life for us after the bad men. Even some good men around. So hang on, Amber. Eventually you get past the shock, then you get past the anger, and then life begins again. I hope yours turns out as well as mine has."

"I hope so, too."

"Well," Hope continued, "when I arrived here I was at the end of my rope, emotionally and financially. All I knew was I had to figure out a way to take care of my baby. That was all I had left to hang on to. You hang on to that, Amber." Then she rose.

"Cash insists our younger daughter go to preschool because he doesn't want her to miss the social interaction like she would out on the ranch. But this is also my free time to catch up with errands, and I only have a few hours." She turned and pulled a piece of paper off the memo pad on the refrigerator door and scribbled down her number. "Here's my number. Don't be afraid to call for any reason at all."

Then she grabbed her jacket, patted Amber's shoulder and headed out the door.

Feeling almost as if a whirlwind had blown through, Amber sat eating crackers, and as her stomach settled, she even felt the return of some appetite.

She liked Hope and she could understand why Wyatt had confided in her. She looked at the business card on the table and reached for the phone hanging on the wall. She needed to do this. Playing ostrich wasn't good for her or the baby who was finally becoming real to her.

After ten minutes she had an appointment later in the week with the doctor, Joy Castor. She wrote it on the back of the card and then went out to the foyer to tuck it in her purse. That would make Wyatt happy, she thought. In the meantime, she needed to shake herself out of the mental stasis that seemed to be enveloping her again. She'd quit a job, packed up her life and come running to a friend, but everything else seemed to have shut down. No thoughts for the future, no plans in the works, and for the first time the denial about her pregnancy seemed to be waning.

So what next? She wished she could think of something. Anything. God, she needed a plan. Right now the future looked empty and threatening, and it didn't seem to be getting any better.

Midafternoon, just as she was deciding she couldn't hibernate in this house and at least needed to get out for a walk, the doorbell rang again. Now who had Wyatt sent?

She opened to the door and faced a young woman somewhere near her age with upswept hair wearing a dress and heels. She was used to seeing that in the city, but she already had the sense it wasn't that common around here. She thought of Wyatt wearing jeans under his robe, and most of the people he'd talked to in the courtroom yesterday. They hadn't even dressed up for that.

"May I help you?" she asked.

"So you're the new girlfriend."

Shock rammed Amber. She wasn't usually thrown off balance easily with the law. This was a side of the world she had only minimal acquaintance with. "I'm sorry?"

"Wyatt's new girlfriend," the woman said. "I heard about you."

Already? "Um…we're just old friends."

"Sure. Well, I'm Ellie Rich, his former fiancée. I just wanted to see who was stupid enough to fall for that guy. Big mistake, lady. He's all nice on the outside and ugly on the inside. Or maybe you're his new cover story."

Then the woman turned and walked away, leaving Amber standing there with the door open and hardly aware of the chilly air. Ellie climbed into her car and drove away fast enough to leave a little rubber behind. The instant she disappeared around the corner, Wyatt's car appeared from the opposite direction and pulled into the driveway.

Abruptly aware that she was getting cold, Amber pivoted and reached for her jacket but didn't close the door. Wyatt climbed out, clad in jeans and a blue sweater, paused to look at her standing in the open doorway, concern creasing his brow, then loped up the sidewalk and onto the porch.

"Something wrong?" he asked.

"Ellie. At least she said she was."

His face darkened. "Damn that woman. You're shivering. Let's get inside."

He urged her into the foyer and closed the door. "You look like you need a hot drink." A gentle hand on the small of her back urged her into the kitchen.

"I'm fine. There's coffee. Your friend Hope made it earlier. I think it's still good." In some crazy way, it was as if she were pulling out of her body, standing at a distance from everything. How strange. How very weird.

"I'm not worried about coffee," he said, an edge to his voice. "I'm worried about *you*." Without another word, he pulled out ingredients. "Cocoa coming up."

Amber sat at the table again, trying to figure out what was wrong with her. It was as if she was removed from everything, but she was sure she hadn't felt that way until just recently. Maybe since she got here. It was weird, as if nearly everything inside her had shut down. Before, she'd put a few matters on hold to deal with later. But all of a sudden she felt as if everything was on hold. She felt numb, almost disinterested, after her teary meltdown just yesterday.

As soon as Wyatt had the cocoa simmering, he got himself some coffee and joined her at the table. "Ellie didn't say anything to upset you, did she?"

"I think I'm past getting upset about anything." A blessing perhaps, but not normal. "She basically told me she was your ex, accused me of being your new girlfriend, or alternatively your new cover story, then she left."

"I'm sorry," he said. Reaching across the table, he clasped her hand briefly. His touch felt surprisingly warm and pleasant.

"Don't be sorry. I'm quite sure you didn't ask her to stop by. That's all on her."

"Regardless, you didn't need it. I don't believe that woman." Rising, he went to stir the simmering cocoa. "It's been over a year. You'd think she would have moved on."

"I don't know. I seem to be having trouble moving at all."

In a flash he was squatting beside her. "What's wrong, Amber? Are you sick?"

She shook her head a little. "I'm fine. Some morning sickness, but Hope helped with that. No, it's like… it's like everything has shut down. I'm numb. I can't think. I've got to plan a future, and it feels as if my brain went on vacation. My emotions, too." As busy as she'd been in the last month, maybe this had been happening all along and she just hadn't noticed it. Was she losing her mind?

He nodded and touched her shoulder lightly. "Maybe you've been through all the emotional turmoil you can stand for a while. Your mind and emotions might just be forcing a holiday on you."

"Holiday?" Despite her oddly removed state, she almost laughed. "Some holiday."

"A rest, then. Maybe you just need a break from it all. Or maybe you can't deal with it all at once. There's been an awful lot to deal with."

"Maybe."

"No maybe about it," he said. "You were awfully clinical when you called me and told me you were in trouble. It's a bit of self-protection going on here. I hope it doesn't all just crash in at once."

She gazed into his face, reading his concern but more, his kindness. He'd always accepted her just as she was, and he was doing it right now. Some part of her acknowledged that she ought to feel a whole lot more messed up than she did, but except for that crying fit yesterday, she felt as if her mind and heart were wrapped in cotton. So maybe he was right. Yesterday she had wept and hurt for quite a long time. Then everything had been steadily and slowly stilling inside her. Enough for now.

He touched her cheek, and a pleasant shiver ran through her. Well, at least she could still feel that. It would have been so easy to just fall into his arms. Because she wanted to know what it would feel like to rest her head on his shoulder. To feel his lips on hers. To feel his skin against hers. To feel him filling the emptiness inside her. She'd always wanted to know.

"You did cry yesterday," he reminded her. "Privately, but it was there on your face when you came down for dinner. Take it a step at a time. Now I need to check that cocoa before I scorch it."

He stirred it a few more times while she watched and tried to think of a safe place to go with their conversation. It would be almost impossible to feel any more disconnected than she did right now. Except for one connection, that was. Her desire for him was probably the only part of her that was still awake and responding.

"How was court?" she asked.

"A very interesting bigamy case."

That caught her attention and drove her preoccupation into the background. He filled two mugs with frothy cocoa and put one in front of her. "How could you commit bigamy in a town this size?"

He laughed and sat across from her. "Believe it or not, you can. But not the way you'd expect."

"So what happened?"

"This couple split maybe thirteen years ago. She threw him out and told him she was filing for divorce. So he moved to California, where he got a job and, believe it or not, sent regular child support checks."

"Why believe it or not?"

His smile widened. "It was never ordered by a court. He was just doing what he thought was right."

"I already like him. Then?"

"Then, all these years later he comes back to town. Stops by to see his kids, meets a new woman, they date and after a few months they got married. Supposedly ex-wife hears about the marriage and immediately calls the cops to press bigamy charges. She had never divorced him."

"But…" Her mind boggled. "How did he not know?"

"You're a lawyer, you understand how this works. This guy was poorly educated, never had anything to do with the law until this. My guess is it never occurred to him that he was supposed to get divorce papers to sign, or a decree. Anyway, after listening to all of this, the jury apparently decided that after thirteen years he probably believed he was divorced and therefore didn't intend to commit bigamy."

"And it's an intent crime?"

"That's one of the elements."

"I love it. He must have had a good lawyer, though."

"Public defender," he answered. "And she was good. She kept hammering on the intent part of the crime and how you have to *knowingly* be married to two women at the same time." He laughed quietly. "I enjoyed that trial. I think I enjoyed the outcome even more. That guy was no more intentionally guilty of bigamy than I am. And all those years he paid child support without a court order. I know a lot of men who begrudge it even when a court orders it."

"I've heard plenty of them gripe about it," she agreed. "Honestly, I don't get it. When you dump a spouse you don't dump your kids. Or at least you shouldn't."

"I absolutely agree. I do family court as well, and failure to pay child support is the most frequent type of case to come before me."

She arched a brow, surprised. "You're a jack-of-all-trades."

"Within my jurisdiction, yeah. Look at this place, Amber. I have a couple of magistrates who help deal with the really minor things, but they aren't even lawyers. So I get everything in the area that doesn't need to go to the district court."

"This is so very different," she murmured, even as she realized he had successfully pulled her away from her spiraling concern about being so numb. Maybe he was right. Maybe she just needed a break from it all. God knew, she was weary of feeling overwhelmed, rudderless. Her old life was over. She needed to move on. And apparently she needed some time to do just that. Time that Wyatt was giving her.

Then he asked, "Did you make an appointment?"

"Yeah. For Thursday. You can relax."

"I wasn't uptight," he answered. "So you had morning sickness?"

"I guess that's what it was." She looked down at herself, trying to imagine the child growing inside her. It still seemed so far away, so removed. At two months she could barely see any changes in her body.

"You'll probably find out tomorrow morning." He winked, but this time she didn't even smile back. She had found a safe, quiet place in the middle of the maelstrom her life had become, and right now she didn't want one damn thing to disturb it.

Wyatt was more concerned about her withdrawal than he let on. After yesterday's crying jag upstairs—and yeah, he'd known from the puffiness of her face when she came back downstairs—now this? Like a switch had flipped?

He'd tried to be reassuring about it, but he wasn't at all convinced it was a normal reaction. When he thought about all that had happened to her in the last month or so, he supposed she was entitled to withdraw for a while. It was enough to devastate anyone, and she hadn't allowed herself much time to just sit, cry and brood.

She'd made two incredibly tough decisions, the first to quit the firm, the second to keep her child. Life altering, life shattering.

Yeah, she was entitled to shut down for a while. He just wondered at what point he should start to really worry.

At least she was drinking her cocoa. "I was thinking about roasting a chicken for dinner tonight. Does that sound good to you?"

She nodded. "Very good, actually." Then, just as he started to rise to get the chicken out of the refrigerator, she said, "Ellie."

He sat again. "What about her?"

"She's very pretty."

"Only on the outside," he said, a slight edge in his voice. "I told you."

"I know."

He put his elbows on the table and studied her. "What does it matter what she looks like?"

"It doesn't. It's only that I can't imagine why she came over here. It was pointless. You broke up with her a long time ago. It's just weird that she evidently wanted to say something nasty to me about you."

Ellie was at least outside the circle of Amber's problems, and therefore safe. He got it. Well, if she wanted to talk about that woman, he supposed he could as well. He'd left Ellie in his distant emotional past.

Amber spoke again. "Did she hurt you very badly?"

He hesitated. "At first I was so angry I learned what it means to see red. Asking me to intervene on the charges against her cousin…she should have known me better by then. But no, she thought she could manipulate me into doing something that violated all my principles. That's when I knew what she really thought of me. So later, when I stopped being so angry, yeah, I was hurt. I'd thought I was in love. I'd almost asked that woman to marry me. It took a while for me to just feel grateful she'd pulled that stunt *before* we were married. Or had kids."

"I bet," she said quietly.

"So I escaped by the skin of my teeth." He shook his head and gave her a lopsided smile. "Live and learn. Trite but true. A wise man, namely my dad, once told me that we learn more from our mistakes than we do from getting it right. I'm here to testify that it may not feel like it at the time, but he was right. I learned a lot from that experience."

"Any of it good?"

He reached across the table and took her hand again. Her fingers felt cold. "A lot of it. Give yourself time, Amber. Do you want mittens or another cup of cocoa?"

That at least broke through her frozen state enough to make her smile faintly. "Cocoa, please. I don't know why I feel so cold. I'm sure it's warm enough in here, and it's not like I just came from some southern climate."

He had no answer for that. Maybe she was just run-down. Regardless, he was glad she would see the doc in two days. "It'll warm up in the kitchen soon, because I'm going to turn on the oven. In the meantime, do you want me to get you a wrap? A blanket? A shawl?"

At that she looked up. "You have a *shawl*?"

He laughed. "They used to be quite common, and you have to remember a lot of generations have lived here. Yes, I have a shawl. I have a few of them. Lucky I didn't give them to the church rummage sale, but I can still remember my great-grandmother wearing them. I loved that woman."

"I'd like to hear about her."

"Let me get that shawl and I'll bore you to tears."

Responsive at least, he thought as he dashed upstairs to a storage closet. Distant, but not gone.

There was a cedar closet off the wide hallway. Over the years it had probably stored many things, especially when woolens were so popular and moths a big problem, but now it was down to mostly keepsakes, carefully wrapped in plastic by his mother before she died. Earl and Wyatt had never used it for much, although Earl did have one good wool coat hanging in there from many years ago. Wyatt doubted he'd be able to squeeze into it now.

Most of what was left were items he and his father hadn't been able to part with. It was easy to find one of his great-grandmother's shawls, and he paused a few minutes, lost in memories of her. More than anyone else, she had helped him get through the weeks after his mother's shocking death.

He stroked the shawl with his hand, remembering her wearing it. Suddenly remembering that a long time ago Amber had told him about her aversion to wool. Well, all the rest were wool shawls, with the exception of this one, his favorite. His grandmother had tatted it herself, he was told, and she liked peacocks. This had been tatted out of colorful embroidery silks.

Anyway, it was pretty, and while he cherished it more than the others, it was the only one Amber could wear.

Downstairs, he draped it around Amber's shoulders. "Not wool, but warm anyway, I imagine."

"I seem to be allergic to wool," she replied. "Thank you. It's beautiful."

He didn't tell her that he'd recalled that errant remark from so long ago. He didn't know why, but he felt it might make her uneasy to know she'd made such an impression on him. "My great-grandma tatted it out of some embroidery silk. Every time I look at it I think about time, patience and talent. And I remember she wore it only on Sundays."

He paused to switch the oven on and pulled out a roasting pan, which he oiled. Then he stood at the sink washing the chicken under a stream of cold water. "You just want it plain?"

"That might be safest right now."

He glanced over his shoulder and saw her looking down at the shawl, stroking it with her hand.

"It's so lovely," she said quietly. "Was it fashionable?"

"Now that I can't tell you. I remember her from when she was in her seventies and eighties and I was just a kid. She made me feel special, though. Every time I was with her, I felt wrapped in love."

"You were very fortunate."

From what she had said yesterday, he wondered if she had, even once in her life, felt wrapped in love.

"I was," he agreed. "She used to take me on walks in the summertime for a picnic. She mixed her homemade preserves with powdered sugar to make icing and spread it on graham crackers. Then we'd hike out to the railroad tracks and back. It always seemed like an adventure, even though I could see the town in the distance. I was small, though, so those distances seemed huge."

He buttered the chicken on the outside, then washed his hands. It was a nuisance, getting the butter off, but he'd never found a better way to oil the chicken, and he liked the way the butter tasted. He skipped his usual preference for some paprika and just lightly salted it. Then into the oven. When he turned around, drying his hands on a towel, he saw Amber sitting with her chin in her hand looking quite pensive.

"Something the matter?" he asked.

"Just thinking about how nice those picnics must have been for you. I'd have liked to do something like that."

"What kinds of things did you do as a child?" He hoped it hadn't all been as bleak as she'd sounded yesterday, pushed every step of the way by ambitious parents.

"Normal stuff, I guess. My grandparents were gone by the time I was five, and I don't remember them well. Except they never seemed like grandparents."

"How so?" He moved closer to the table.

"I don't know. It was like visiting people I didn't know very well, and I always had to be on my best behavior. Not one of them made cookies." She gave a mirthless laugh. "I see that stuff on TV and wonder where those grandparents are. Your great-grandmother sounds like she might have fit the bill."

"She did. Of them all, she was my favorite. But maybe she'd reached a time in life where other things didn't preoccupy her. I guess she spoiled me in a lot of ways."

She moved her head a little. "Maybe every child deserves someone to spoil them. I get that parents can't afford to, but other people can."

"How much of a monster do you want to raise?"

At that he finally drew a laugh from her. Was she coming back? He hoped so. "So nobody spoiled you?"

She twisted her hands. "I guess that depends on what you mean by spoiling. I was luckier than a lot of kids. A stable home, concerned parents, never hungry, always well dressed. Yeah, I was spoiled in a different way."

"By helicopter parents?"

Her eyes widened. "What is that?"

"Parents who get involved in every aspect in a child's life, always there to dive in and straighten a crooked path, to defend a kid against any kind of trouble at all. Overly involved, I guess."

She appeared to think about that. "I don't know," she said finally. "I wouldn't say they were overprotective. On the other hand…" She shook her head. "I didn't have a whole lot of opportunity to get in trouble. Guess I just made up for that."

"Big-time," he said with a wink. "Seriously, Amber, we all make mistakes, some big, some small, but we all make them."

"This is a humdinger."

He hesitated. While he wasn't much for Pollyannas, he could sometimes be one. "Maybe someday it'll look like the best thing that could have happened. No guarantees, of course, but you might find that life with a child makes you very happy, and you might find another position that doesn't consume your entire life. Just spitballing here. I don't expect you to believe it."

She looked down at her twisting fingers. "I don't make mistakes. The first thing I have to learn to live with is that apparently I do make them. Then maybe I can move on."

He felt truly bad for her. There hadn't been a whole lot of time for her to adjust to anything and being used that way by the jackass at her firm was something that might leave bruises, if not scars, for a long time to come.

"And no talking to your father?"

"Not yet," she said, her head snapping up. "I can already write the lecture in my head. I don't need to hear it."

God, that was a statement, he thought. And it sure explained why she'd called him rather than her father. "I'm not saying you have to call."

He wished he had some clue how to help her with all this. He'd split up families in court, usually for damn good reasons, but it was usually painful for all involved, no matter how valid the reasons.

"I'm selfish," she blurted.

Surprised, he didn't answer, just waited. What in the world?

"I realized yesterday that I've been the center of the universe my entire life. My parents put me there, and I believed it. Anyway, yesterday it struck me that I had no business calling you, without a thought for what you might have going on in your life, and running straight to you for help. Then you mentioned your election coming up... I never thought of you, Wyatt."

"Yes, you did. You called me. Couldn't have paid me a higher compliment. So relax."

"How can I relax when your ex shows up at the door ready to start an old battle, one that doesn't affect me but could certainly hurt you? What happens if someone notices me going to the obstetrician? Someone will undoubtedly start speculating that you got me pregnant. None of this is going to help with your election!"

Well, the withdrawal was gone temporarily, but he didn't like this turn of events at all. "I don't care what people think."

"You have to," she said hotly. "You're a freaking judge!"

Wow. He tried to remember if he'd ever seen this much fire in Amber. No, he was sure he hadn't. Fear, nerves, humor…but never fiery. Always the good girl. Now this? He hated to admit it, but he rather liked it.

"It's okay, Amber."

"No, it's not okay. Most especially it's not okay that I dropped myself on you without a thought to the consequences to you. I need to leave as soon as possible."

"And go where?" he asked quietly.

She averted her face. Clearly she had no answer. And apparently he hadn't convinced her that she was truly welcome here. He wasn't worried about the election. However that went, he wasn't that involved. He liked being a judge, but he'd liked working as a lawyer, too. His whole life didn't hang on one thing.

But hers did now. She'd just given up everything, lost everything she had worked for. Maybe she thought a career change would be as troubling for him as hers was for her.

He was still trying to think of ways to reassure her when the doorbell rang. The sound struck him as poorly timed in the worst way. Amber needed something right now, and that wouldn't come from answering the door.

But before he could stir to go see who it was, he heard the door open. In an instant he knew who had arrived.

Just what they needed right now: his dad.

Chapter Six

"Do I smell chicken roasting?" Earl asked cheerfully as he entered the kitchen. At once his sharp dark eyes measured the situation.

Wyatt figured he and Amber looked pretty tense, and Earl wouldn't miss it. He tried to divert his father. "Are you inviting yourself to dinner?" It had happened a hundred times before, but not at a time like this. Earl knew he had company.

"Wouldn't miss it. Alma's gone to visit her sister. This must be your friend Amber."

Amber stared at him, clearly wondering who Earl was and why he had just walked in and invited himself to dinner.

"Amber, this is my father, Earl. Dad, my friend Amber."

"From law school, right?" Earl said, offering his hand. Amber shook it without speaking, merely offering a faint smile.

Earl pulled out a chair and sat, eyeing Amber. "You look a lot younger than I would have expected."

Wyatt wondered how to handle this. His dad was probing, and like a good lawyer he probably wouldn't stop his cross-examination until he was satisfied. "Amber started law school young, Dad. And I don't think she appreciates your inquisitor's tactics."

Earl twisted his head to look at his son. "She can stand it. She's a lawyer, too."

At that Amber made a muffled sound, but her face revealed nothing. Earl studied her for a few more seconds as he shrugged his jacket off and let it drape over the back of the chair. He paused a moment to smooth his gray hair, then he charged in again. "I'm surprised I didn't meet you before. For friends of long standing, you two sure haven't spent any time together."

Wyatt wanted to groan. He shouldn't have to explain anything, nor should Amber. "We kept in touch, Dad. Now drop it, please."

Amber spoke at last, surprising him by the firmness of her tone. Earl must have awakened the lawyer in her. "I was two years behind your son, Mr. Carter. He went his way when he graduated and I went mine, to St. Louis and then Chicago. Unfortunately, my work didn't leave me any time for visiting old friends or taking holidays."

"A good reason to avoid those big firms," Earl remarked. "But you'll probably be bored to death here." He twisted again to look at Wyatt. "What are you serving with the chicken?"

"I haven't fleshed out the menu yet."

"I like that boxed stuffing mix. Or how about yellow rice? I realize you won't get to show off by opening a box for your friend here, but it's good stuff."

That elicited a welcome laugh from Amber. Earl's gaze settled on her again. "I heard you met Ellie today."

Amber's eyes widened. "You heard about that? She was only here for a minute."

"Word gets around. Did Wyatt tell you about their breakup? He should have told more people."

"Dad…" Wyatt was ready to throw up his hands. He wished he could ask his father to leave before he managed to upset Amber, but…well, it was his dad's house, too.

"Only a bit," Amber said.

Wyatt spoke. "Don't encourage him, Amber."

"Why not?" she asked. "The woman came by, obviously with an agenda. Maybe I should know more about it."

Earl fixed her with his gaze. "I could like you. Of course she had an agenda. She's always had an agenda. First it was to marry one of the most powerful men in the county, one who owned one of the biggest houses and had a social life with the movers and shakers… if you can call them that around here. Big dreams, that girl."

Wyatt sighed and gave up. He poured his father some coffee and joined them at the table. "I'm a slightly large frog in a very small pond, Dad. No more important than anyone else."

"I'm glad your ego didn't grow," Earl said, "but the simple fact is you're a judge. That's important, however small the pond." He turned back to Amber. "So did he tell you Ellie wanted him to dismiss charges against her cousin?"

Amber nodded.

"Well, of course he wouldn't do it. Not that he couldn't have, but Wyatt, I'm proud to say, has very strong principles and ethics. So of course he said no. And of course he realized that he'd almost gotten engaged to exactly the wrong kind of woman. Although she certainly claimed to have been his fiancée. The woman couldn't tell the truth if her life depended on it. Now while Wyatt probably wouldn't tell a soul this, *I* know how deeply hurt he was."

"Dad…"

"Let me continue. So Ellie sets about trying to sabotage him by telling everyone they broke up because he's gay. Wyatt doesn't care about that. But some folks do. Only time will tell how much damage that woman managed to do to him in some quarters. Now he's coming up for retention."

"I know," Amber said quietly. "I was saying just a little while ago that I need to leave so I don't cause any problems with that."

"Well, I was thinking the same thing," Earl said. "Before. But with Ellie in the mix…do Wyatt a favor, Amber. Stay."

Wyatt shook his head, wondering what kind of machination his father was up to. "My election prospects aren't Amber's problem, Dad."

"Maybe not, but if she's a friend, she'll care anyway. She can put any rumors to rest even if Ellie tries to wind it up again."

Wyatt clenched his teeth. His dad wouldn't let go of that, couldn't get it through his head that if people were going to choose a judge based on something as irrelevant as his social life, then he wasn't sure he wanted to be a judge any longer.

Amber spoke slowly. "I'm aware of the concern. But I don't want to be a new one."

Earl sighed. "How could a woman staying with my son be as big a problem as…"

Amber interrupted. "I'm pregnant. And not by Wyatt."

"Well, no one needs to know…"

"From what I gather about this town, some will when I see the obstetrician on Thursday."

Wyatt had the rare pleasure of seeing his father shut up.

"Anyway," Amber said, "just before you arrived, I was telling Wyatt that I should leave soon so I don't somehow become an issue in this election. Ellie said something about me being a cover story. Do you really think my mere presence here could change that perception in those who believe what Ellie said originally? And if people start to believe that he got me pregnant and we're not married, how does that help?"

"Damn it," said Wyatt, "this is the twenty-first century and I'm not going to be guided by Victorian rules. Period. What's more, Amber, you have no place to go from here yet. No plan. You were blindsided and I offered to help. To hell with everything else."

"That's my son," said Earl, smiling faintly. "Full steam ahead and damn the torpedoes."

"I wouldn't have imagined that," Amber replied. "He's so very thoughtful, contained, even tempered. He's full of good sense."

"Usually," Earl said with a significant look at his son.

Wyatt was losing his usually even temper. "Dad,

just stay out of this. Amber needs a friend. I'm her friend. I told you before that I'm not worried about the election. Period. So just leave it alone."

Amber looked at Earl. "From what I saw yesterday in court, he's a very good judge."

"Most folks seem to think so."

"Then what's the problem," Wyatt demanded.

"There's just so much you can thumb your nose at people."

"The people I'm thumbing my nose at will probably wind up in my courtroom sooner or later charged with something!"

"Ha," said Earl. "I was beginning to wonder if being a judge had deprived you of your passion." He turned back to Amber. "He hasn't been told yet, but he's getting the endorsement of the police association and the chamber hereabouts. And a few others. It's going to come out in the local paper and news in about ten days. Plenty of endorsements. But endorsements alone don't win an election. Then there's that group of religious fringe types run by old Loftis. They don't like you at all."

"A whole thirty of them," Wyatt said. "Can we change the subject, please? This is nothing for Amber to worry about."

"I'd like that yellow rice with the chicken," Earl said, then looked at Amber. "If you don't mind."

"It sounds good to me."

Wyatt seldom felt off balance, but his father and Amber had succeeded in making him feel that way. He was used to making his own decisions, choosing his own path, and now it seemed these two were conspiring. He supposed they thought they were helping, he certainly didn't think either of them wished him ill, but... Damn, it was *his* election. A lot about Conard County still resided in an earlier time, but that was part of the place's charm. He would rise or fall by it, and he accepted that.

The chicken began sizzling in the oven, adding more of its delicious aroma to the air. He glanced at the clock and decided it was going to be an early dinner. Which meant his father would be out of here soon after, before he did something to upset Amber.

He was very much afraid his father would, too. It wasn't that he was a hurtful man, but all these years of practicing law had taught him how to guard his tongue, as well as how to speak out when he believed it necessary. In protective father mode, he could be quite harsh.

"So," Earl said as Wyatt pulled out the rice cooker, "Wyatt says you were blindsided?"

Wyatt stiffened. *Why don't you poke a little harder, Dad? Maybe you can make her cry again.*

"Sort of," Amber said. "A married partner who said he was getting a divorce but wasn't. And an unexpected contraceptive failure."

Earl nodded. "Relax, son, I'm not here to hurt your friend."

Maybe not, Wyatt thought, placing the cooker on the island near an electrical outlet. Then again...

"Old story," Earl said. "If history were a record of men lying to women, it would be a thousand times as long."

Relief washed through Wyatt as he heard Amber laugh quietly. "You might be right, Earl."

"Course I am. Now, Wyatt, he's often right. I'm *always* right."

Another laugh. Then quietly, "Earl, I really don't want to cause him any trouble."

"You won't," Earl said decisively. "Made up my mind. You stay put and I'll get out ahead of the gossip. It can be done."

"I'm still here," Wyatt reminded his father acidly. Cripes, a person would have thought he was running for the presidency, not circuit judge.

Earl turned his head. "My gosh, you still are. Cook away, boy. I got a lady to get to know." Then he leaned toward Amber and said the last thing Wyatt wanted her to hear. "Never could figure out why Wyatt didn't date you in law school. He called me every weekend and we talked more about you than we did about his studies."

Wyatt wanted to sink as his dad turned to him. "Think I didn't remember, son? Of course I did. You were sweet on this lady." Then he looked at Amber. "Didn't you want to date him?"

Wyatt wanted to strangle his father. But Amber smiled faintly. "Very much, Earl," she answered. "But he thought I was too young for him."

"Funny," said Earl, "how that matters less as we get older. How much longer until dinner?"

Amber really liked Earl. She could easily see how he might annoy Wyatt no end sometimes, but he obviously loved his son. Coming from that place, he could be forgiven a great deal, not that he'd really done anything wrong yet. And she could see where Wyatt had gotten much of his remarkable personality. Not all of it, of course, but quite a bit of it.

She wished she'd had a father like Earl, so involved in protecting his child. Her own father had been rather distant and had measured her by her achievements. Earl, while pushing about this election, seemed to want only what was truly best for Wyatt.

Nor had she minded hearing that Earl thought Wyatt had been sweet on her all those years ago. Wyatt probably had, but it made Amber feel good.

During dinner, which was delicious, she asked, "Did you always want Wyatt to be a judge?"

"I wouldn't have cared if he wanted to do something besides the law, though I have to admit I often talked to him about joining my practice. But if that was my dream and not his, that was okay by me."

Wyatt spoke. "Then why are you so wound up about this election?"

"Because you enjoy it, son. You enjoy being a judge even more than you enjoyed practicing law. I see it in you. Hell, you might become a district judge eventually, if that's what you want. The point here is I'm not going to let that nasty woman ruin something you love. Period."

Then Earl surprised Wyatt by turning the conversation to the practice of law, comparing notes with Amber. Just two lawyers talking about their work, about the differences between small-town solo practice and working for large firms.

As they ate, Wyatt kept fairly quiet, watching something grow between Amber and Earl. Some kind of connection, although he wasn't sure what type. But Earl had always been good with people, Wyatt a little less so. As Earl had pointed out more than once, Wyatt could get stubborn when he shouldn't.

Wyatt acknowledged his own stubborn streak and tried to rein it in, but he was well aware that opposition stiffened him, even if he was wrong. Every time his dad tried to tell him he needed to worry about the election, he got his back up.

Idiot, he told himself. His dad was right—he did love being a judge. Losing the position wouldn't kill him, but it would disappoint him. Yet here he was, holding the line because he refused to bend about his personal life, because he honestly thought his personal life shouldn't decide how people voted for him as a judge.

Yet what could he do about it? He couldn't stop rumors if people wanted to believe them. But he also didn't want Amber being used in some way. Certainly not as the cover story that Ellie had suggested and which Earl now seemed to be seconding.

He couldn't say much about it right now, because Earl and Amber were deeply involved in their conversation about being lawyers. Amber appeared to be cheering up a bit, returning from wherever she had been when he came home. Irritated as he might be with his father's butting in, he was grateful that it helped Amber.

At last Earl seemed to have gotten what he wanted, and as usual skedaddled before the cleanup. That had always amused Wyatt. From the time his mother had passed, Earl had hired someone to do all the cooking and cleaning for him. Earl might do repairs around the house, but he had apparently maintained a very old-fashioned notion of gender roles.

Wyatt didn't mind, however. He enjoyed cooking, and cleaning was no bother. He had a crew in twice a month to do this monstrosity of a house from top to bottom simply because of the time involved, but he had no objection to doing any of the work himself. Least of all cleaning up after a meal.

Amber offered to help, and rather than make her feel like some kind of burden, he welcomed her. The job was a little more confusing because she didn't yet know her way around the kitchen, but it gave them an opportunity to talk about the most innocuous things, like how to put the remaining chicken away and did he want to save that little bit of yellow rice. Boring, safe stuff.

But then they were done and the long evening stretched ahead. Instead of leaving her to her own devices, he asked her if she wanted to join him in the office. He had some more work to do, prep for upcoming cases, motions to review. She accepted with alacrity, then asked if there was some way she could hook up her laptop.

Well, of course there was. He soon had her wired in and settled in a deep armchair with an ottoman. Ten minutes after he started reading the motions in front of him, he looked up to see that she had fallen asleep.

He was glad to see her resting, but it made him a bit uncomfortable, too. In the lamplight, he couldn't fail to notice that as attractive as she had been a decade ago, she had grown even more so.

She was a woman who would have caught his eye if she'd been a stranger. But she was no stranger. She was living under his roof, and he'd better submerge the impulses she was waking in him.

Sitting there while she slept, he could admit that he wanted her. Hell, he'd wanted her all those years ago but felt it would be taking advantage of her. Maybe at some level he'd never stopped wanting her.

So while his body responded, his mind put on the brakes. If he'd thought he would be taking advantage of her all those years ago, the current situation hadn't improved things. Not while she was so wounded and so dependent on him. It wouldn't be right.

He forced his attention back to the papers on his desk, but instead of seeing the motions, he could only see Amber.

In two short days, she seemed to have filled his life.

Amber awoke slowly, gradually becoming aware of her surroundings. She was still in Wyatt's office at the rear of the house. Lined in floor-to-ceiling book-shelves that held a lot of beautifully bound books, it was warmly lit. A heavy burgundy curtain covered the only window. His desk was large, made of mahogany, the computer on it looking out of place in a room that appeared to have come from a different era. A welcoming room.

Wyatt's face was illuminated by the glow of his computer screen. Her own computer had been removed from her lap and set on a table beside her, its screen black as it slept.

Wyatt, she thought sleepily, must be verifying the legal references in the motions he was reviewing. The light on his face flickered a bit as he changed pages.

She was curled up in the wing-back chair, quite comfortable, and staring at Wyatt felt pleasant. All those years ago, she'd had a crush on him, hardly admitted it even to herself. Then he'd left and they'd kept in touch only loosely as life had taken her down paths far from his. But she remembered those feelings now and felt their rebirth.

Her eyelids at half-mast, she watched him and wondered. What would it be like to rest her head on his shoulder and inhale his scents? What would it be like to feel his lips on hers, his hands exploring her secrets? A trickle of barely tamped desire began to grow into a river inside her.

Was she losing it? If so, she didn't care. He'd done not one thing to make her feel she was any more than a lost kitten he'd taken in, a stray. Kind, friendly, allowing her to make claims on a friendship from ages ago as if it had been only yesterday. Despite what Earl had said about Wyatt being sweet on her all those years ago, that didn't seem to be true now.

Earl's concerns floated back to her, and she decided that Wyatt might not be making the best decisions for himself. Yes, he'd come riding to her rescue. He'd always been a bit of a white knight in her experience, but he was putting an awful lot at risk. His ex-girlfriend apparently still harbored enough of a grudge that she wanted to hurt him, and what better way than by costing him an election?

Wyatt could dismiss those concerns, but Amber discovered she couldn't. She had dealt with enough clients to know that taking the high road wasn't always the best solution. In fact, those who were willing to sink to the lowest level often took advantage of those who refused to.

Was he really that unconcerned?

She stirred and discovered that he'd draped a dark blue throw over her legs to keep her warm. He looked up.

"Sleep well?" he asked.

The words popped out without warning. "We should get engaged."

Under other circumstances she might have enjoyed seeing Wyatt flummoxed. After all, he was always so controlled and in charge of himself. But she heard her own words on the silent air, took in his expression and wondered what devil had possessed her.

"Sheesh," she said.

The stunned expression on his face began to slip into amusement. "I hope it was a nice dream."

For some reason that irritated her. "I wasn't dreaming about you," she said sharply. Or had she been? Any dream had vanished like a wisp of smoke, whatever it had been. But certainly those words had popped out of her as if they had begun somewhere earlier.

They *had* begun earlier. With his father. With the feeling she might cost him something very important by staying with him as a friend, especially if people saw her going to the obstetrician. Maybe Earl *could* get out in front of it, explain that she had left a broken relationship in Chicago and was indeed just visiting for a short while. But how would that help stop the viciousness that Ellie was spreading? While she agreed with Wyatt that it shouldn't matter to people, she knew that in the real world such things *did* matter.

"Did Earl get to you?" he asked finally.

"I guess he did."

"Don't let him."

"Actually," she said, stiffening her spine, "I thought your father made some good points. I saw you in the courtroom. You're a good judge, Wyatt. Very good. People here are lucky to have a judge like you, and you love it. So it just seemed to me that since I'm going to be here awhile, we could get engaged, turn the gossip around and then break up eventually. It's not a big deal for me."

He was silent for a while, steepling his fingers and sitting back in his chair. "I don't like pretense," he said finally. "I appreciate your generosity, but…" He shook his head.

All of a sudden she felt scalded by shame. Maybe she was, in a different way, no better than Ellie. Proposing to live a lie? Of course he would object. "I'm sorry. I know you better than that."

"I'm sure you do," he said quietly. "You weren't fully awake, and my father is probably responsible for your thoughts running in that direction. He was sure trying."

She wished she could hide her face, but she had more backbone than that. "Was he?"

"In an indirect way, yes. It's okay, Amber. You're just trying to help, and he was busy planting ideas that you could. He can be subtle, sometimes, but never say he doesn't understand the human psyche. With a different upbringing he'd probably have been a great con man."

She gasped. "That's how you see your father?"

He laughed quietly. "No, but I've had a lot of years to get to know him. He'd never con anyone. But he does know how to, um, get people moving in a direction he wants. Not exactly manipulative. Sometimes I think he doesn't even know he's doing it. It just comes naturally."

"It'd be a useful skill with a jury," she admitted.

"Well, that's what we lawyers try to do in a trial. Make a jury see the case favorably for our clients.

Nothing wrong with that. The other side is working just as hard to make everything look bad for us. So Earl is good at what he does."

"Well, I'm still sorry. I hope I didn't offend you."

He smiled. "I was more worried about trying to find a way to say no that wouldn't offend *you*. I know you well enough to be reasonably certain you weren't thinking of your offer in the way I took it."

"No," she admitted, looking down and picking at the blanket over her legs. "Not for a second did I see it as a lie, though obviously it would have been. So I guess you were right when you said I wasn't fully awake."

"How *did* you see it?"

Her blush returned. "Well, the part about being engaged to you sounded pretty good. The part about breaking it off didn't sound good at all."

A hearty laugh escaped him. "Thanks for the honesty. I wouldn't mind being engaged to you, either. If it were real. So there we are."

Yes, there they were, Amber thought. He turned back to his work, and she reached for her laptop to find something to get her mind to a safe harbor.

Because it was true she wouldn't mind being engaged to him. She thought she'd like it a whole lot. But there was just one little obstacle to that kind of happiness: another man's baby.

After that little scene, Wyatt could no longer concentrate on the legal motions in front of him. He'd had trouble earlier because he was responding to her as a man, and that kind of sexual response was always distracting. People distracted by those urges got themselves into a pickle sometimes, as he saw so often in family court.

But they were still distracting, he still kept feeling a desire to make love with her, and…her suggestion of an engagement had acted like a match in tinder. The man who sat on a bench wearing an impressive robe and looking down at a courtroom full of people while dispensing justice was still just an ordinary man with ordinary needs.

From the moment he had welcomed her to his home with a hug, he'd been uneasily aware that this situation was going to be difficult. In some ways they didn't know each other very well even after all these years. In others…well, the passion he'd never allowed to blossom with her was still there, like a seedling that had just poked its head up to the sun. It wanted to grow and spread.

He didn't believe in pretense, but the idea of trying out an engagement with her didn't repel him. The trying out was different and could be accomplished by that famous old ritual called dating.

Amused by the direction of his thoughts and the constant background hum of desire in his body, he glanced up to see Amber studiously staring at her computer. He'd made her uncomfortable, and while he'd tried to smooth it over for her, he was sure she was still wondering what had possessed her. Experienced lawyers rarely just blurted things.

And while he'd blamed it on his dad in order to make her less embarrassed, the truth was Earl hadn't in even the slightest way suggested a pretend engagement. He thought Amber should hang around, not leave, said he was going to get out in front of the gossip, but Wyatt knew his dad well enough to be sure the man wouldn't lie. As for mentioning to Amber that Wyatt had been sweet on her all those years ago… Well, Wyatt honestly believed Earl hadn't had an ulterior motive. It was probably his father's attempt to make Amber feel comfortable about staying.

Which was the other thing about Earl. Wyatt didn't really see him as capable of conning anyone, but he had a good instinct for saying things in a way that would lead others in the direction he wanted.

Still, he hadn't tried to manipulate anyone today. In fact, it was kind of interesting to see where Amber's mind had taken their before-dinner discussion. Evidently she felt a need to act, not just sit back and let matters take their own course.

He forced his gaze back to the motions in front of him. He wasn't going to take advantage of Amber. She was down on her luck and in an awful situation. Nor was he going to let anyone else use her.

He believed his father truly understood that. And if Ellie tried to drag Amber into her gossip war, she was going to be one sorry woman.

Chapter Seven

Amber's appointment with the obstetrician was at four in the afternoon that Thursday. To her surprise, Wyatt wanted to go with her.

"But...that might cause even more talk!"

He arched a brow at her. "So? You're staying with me. And if she has any special directions about diet and so on, maybe I need to hear it."

She threw up a hand, feeling at once frustrated and touched. "You'll drive me mad, Wyatt. Women do this on their own all the time."

"I know, and I'm quite sure you can do it all by yourself. But you don't need to while you're staying with me, and I'd really appreciate it if you'd let me in."

"Let you in?" Confused, she stared at him. They were standing by the front door, ready to go out, and things had just taken a strange turn.

"You're going to have a baby. I get that single mothers succeed all the time. Women are strong. I've seen it, I've heard the arguments and… I'm still feeling a responsibility toward you and this child."

She felt her jaw drop. "To the child? This baby isn't even yours!"

"I know. But that doesn't mean I can't take an interest its father won't take. Or that I don't feel a responsibility toward it."

"God, do you feel responsible for everything?"

One corner of his mouth lifted. "Only for those things I can do something about."

Realizing that if she climbed into her own car and drove off by herself he'd probably just follow her—this wasn't the first time she'd seen signs that he could be stubborn—she gave in. As he drove her to the office, she even had to admit there was a tiny bit of comfort in his caring enough to do this.

Her future yawned in front of her like a huge gulf that held nothing. She was having trouble imagining that in about seven months there'd be a baby in her life. She was getting closer to it, but it still seemed…like someone else's dream. Maybe this visit today would make it feel more real.

Regardless, she decided as they wound along the autumn streets of Conard City, it was nice to have Wyatt with her. She wasn't alone. He'd made it clear that she didn't *have* to be alone, even though this mess was mostly her responsibility.

And in his usual way he was going right ahead and involving himself. The way he had when they'd first met at the law school. He'd only talked to her for a few minutes before he was volunteering to help her with her studies in any way she needed. And far better than the other guys who'd approached her trying to wangle her phone number or suggest they meet, Wyatt had simply given her his own name and phone number. No pressure. *You need some help, call me.*

He'd meant it, too. The first time they'd met for a study session had been in the library. After that they'd sometimes met at other places, growing from tutor and student to friends until it finally hadn't seemed at all out of place to occasionally do something else together.

She'd always felt safe with him, certain that he didn't have some ulterior motive. And then he'd graduated and left for the navy. Only in his absence did she realize how much care he'd taken of her.

Now he was doing it again. She smiled faintly as she looked out the car window, forgetting all her troubles for a few minutes. Wyatt. He'd always been remarkable.

Too bad he'd never acted on his interest in her back then. Too bad he wasn't acting now.

Or maybe she was sending all the wrong signals to him. Maybe she always had.

Then she drew herself up short. How many more problems did she need to add to her life? She'd already done a pretty effective job of hashing it up. Why ruin a perfectly good relationship?

The doctors' office was in a small medical center right near the community hospital.

"This is it," Wyatt said. "Pretty good care from such a small institution."

She hesitated before getting out of the car. "I want to see the doctor by myself."

"You don't think I'd follow you into the exam room, do you? But if there are any instructions…"

She interrupted, giving in. "I get it. You can talk to her after."

"Thank you."

She glanced at him, wondering if he was being sarcastic, but his expression appeared sincere. Well, he *had* pushed himself into the middle of this, and Wyatt wasn't an insensitive dolt. She'd protested, he'd pressed, and he was surely aware that the doctor didn't have to tell him one thing…and wouldn't without her permission.

She had to admit, however, it felt a whole lot better to walk into that office with him at her side. She was nervous about this, although she couldn't exactly say why. She'd had pelvic exams before. This wouldn't be much different.

And yet it was, but she couldn't put her finger on why.

Apparently he sensed her discomfort, because he surprised her by taking her hand and giving it a gentle squeeze before she walked up to the counter to check in. Then he sat in one of the waiting room chairs, and by the time she finished at the counter, he was in conversation with a young woman near her age.

"Amber, this is Julie Archer. She's having her first, too."

Julie had a warm smile and beautiful auburn hair. "Nice to meet you, Amber. Wyatt says you're an old friend of his. I thought I'd meet you Saturday night, but this is a pleasant surprise. How long will you be in town?"

"I'm not sure," Amber answered honestly. "I'm between jobs, and Wyatt's being very generous."

At that moment, a door to the side of reception opened. "Julie? Doctor's ready for you."

Julie smiled warmly at Amber. "I'm sure we'll talk more."

"I hope so." Then someone else in scrubs appeared to give Amber a clipboard full of questions to fill out. Medical history. But as she stared at it, she remembered what Julie had said. "Why would I meet her Saturday night?" she asked.

"I'm having a few friends over, remember? You don't have to attend."

But clearly he'd mentioned Amber. Dang, she thought as she tried to focus on the questionnaire. Was she going to be a bug under a microscope?

"Just a few friends," he said again. "I think you'll like them, and if you stay awhile you won't feel as much like the stranger in a strange land."

She doubted that. Since Tom, there wasn't a day when she didn't feel like a stranger to everything she'd known.

Except Wyatt. After the first brief awkwardness caused by such limited communication over the years, she felt the decade had just slipped away, that she knew him at least as well as she had way back in law school.

Weird. Then she turned her attention to answering all the questions.

The wait for Amber wasn't terribly long, maybe forty-five minutes, but Wyatt had to admit he was a little impatient. Racing around the edges of his thoughts was concern for this child of Amber's. To never know its father? And what about Amber? Sure, women could do this alone. They did all the time, but wouldn't it be easier to have a helpmate, someone to share the burdens? And better yet, the joys.

He'd been looking forward to starting a family as he'd grown more serious with Ellie. Now he'd had one dumped on his doorstep, an old friend he cared about. He hoped he could find a way to persuade Amber to let him be a continuing part of her life and the baby's.

Odd feelings to be having, but it was as if Amber's situation had opened up a surprising place in him. He'd been telling himself he was content and fortunate, and when Ellie had hurt him so deeply, he'd decided it was better to forge ahead alone than to take that risk again. Especially since he could be a bad judge of a woman's character.

Amber's situation should have convinced him he was right. Trusting another person so much, letting them inside so far, only to have them rip out your heart, seemed like a stupid risk to take.

Yet here he was, forming an attachment that could be equally risky. He felt as if the years were slipping away, but he was well aware that Amber couldn't be the young girl he remembered any longer. The years and experience changed people. That should be warning enough, but there was more.

She would be here only temporarily. She had a thirst to do the bigger things in life, hence her decision to go with a large law firm. She clearly wouldn't find enough to stimulate her in a one-horse town like this.

But, damn, he wanted her. The need was growing

with each passing day, and the fact that she was pregnant wasn't stopping it. He supposed he should feel guilty, considering what she was going through and what she still faced. She needed his support and his understanding, not his desire. Hell, she probably felt worse about romantic relationships than he did.

Another woman he vaguely knew arrived for her appointment. He was acutely aware that she did a double take at seeing him here, then smiled and nodded.

And thus began the gossip. He wondered what they'd be saying by tomorrow. Then the receptionist called him. "Judge? You can go back now. First door on the right."

He didn't have to look at the woman—what was her name? He ought to know it—to realize that had sealed the deal. Rockets would be going up in a town where gossip was the only free entertainment. He hoped they enjoyed it.

Setting a smile on his face, he marched through the door and into the office as directed. Dr. Joy Castor sat on the far side of the desk and Amber was seated in one of the two chairs in front of it.

Joy smiled at him. "Hey, Wyatt. Amber tells me you're a buttinsky friend."

"I just want to make sure I do everything right while she's visiting me."

"There speaks a man who's never experienced this before." Joy winked. "Okay, as I told Amber, pregnancy is usually a very healthy, uncomplicated process. A few dos, a few don'ts, unless problems develop, and at this point I don't see anything to worry about. Early days yet, so she should be coming in once a month for the next few months unless she notices a problem of some kind. I gave her a list, so I'm not going to re-cite it."

"Fair enough," Wyatt agreed as relief swept through him.

"Your job," Joy continued, "will be to make sure she takes a walk every day for at least a half hour. Other than that, pamper her all you want." Joy gave a little laugh. "Pampering is a great thing."

When they walked out of the office, the woman who had been there earlier had vanished and no one else was waiting. Wyatt stood by while Amber paid the bill, even though he would have liked to pay it himself.

However, he had a feeling he might have encroached enough for one day. She hadn't even wanted him to come this far.

He stopped by the diner on the way home. "I didn't start dinner," he said. "Want to dine in or should I get takeout?"

She leaned her head back and he saw that she looked tired. "Amber? Are you all right?"

She turned her head, smiling faintly. "I guess I was more uptight about this visit than I realized. I feel drained."

"So eat at home?"

"Please."

It was only Thursday, such a short time since her arrival on Sunday, but she already felt as if she were coming home as she entered Wyatt's house. The min-ute the door closed behind her, she felt cocooned in warmth and safety. Wyatt had always made her feel safe, and she guessed that sense extended to his home.

She *was* tired, though. Hanging her jacket on the coat tree, she followed Wyatt into the kitchen.

"We can eat in here," he said as he began to empty items onto the island, "or I can make you comfy on the living room sofa with a tray table. Your choice."

"The couch might put me to sleep right now, and frankly, I'm more hungry than tired." Barely. She hoped the food would increase her energy level. When he waved her into a chair, she took it and let herself sag a bit. God, she must really have been on pins and needles about this doctor visit. Usually only a trial or a truly difficult client left her feeling this drained. And she'd hardly done a thing today.

Wyatt didn't leave the food in the containers. Instead he scooped just about everything into serving bowls and plates, then invited her to help herself to anything that appealed.

She eyed the amount of food. "You expecting an army?"

He laughed. "No, but leftovers are good, usually, and I didn't bother to ask what you'd like. So a little of everything."

"That sandwich doesn't look *little*," she said.

"No, it's pretty big, but I cut it in half." He poured her a glass of milk and a water for himself, then sat facing her.

"So, okay, what didn't the doc tell me?" he asked as he took half of that huge sandwich. She reached for the salad. Those greens and tomatoes were calling to her like a siren's song.

"Nothing, really," she said. "Life will continue pretty much as normal for a while. Don't wear anything that binds my waist, no more than two cups of coffee a day, take my prenatal vitamins."

"And the morning sickness?"

"I should just avoid any foods that don't appeal to me and otherwise keep crackers beside the bed."

He nodded. "I'll see to it."

She smiled. "It's nothing to worry about unless it gets really bad. So here I am, extremely healthy, and maybe I should try to focus on what I need to do next."

Holding the sandwich in his hand, he raised his gaze to her. "There's no rush, Amber. Let me be perfectly clear about that. You're not putting me out in the least, and I'm actually enjoying getting to know you again. So please, don't feel like you have to rush for any reason. Take your time."

Amber nodded, suddenly unable to speak as her throat tightened. Oh, no, was she going to weep again? Moving between utter numbness and tears was hard to take, swinging back and forth as if she had no control of her emotions. Maybe she didn't. Maybe she was out of control. Maybe it was the pregnancy. Damn, why hadn't she thought to ask the doctor about that?

But Wyatt's generosity had touched her to her very core. She tried to remember the last time anyone had wanted to take care of her without asking anything in return, and she couldn't. Her life had been too work driven, but even her one folly with a man had never made her feel as cared for as Wyatt just had.

"Amber?"

She hardly dared look at him, for fear that he would read her. A lawyer learned to be inscrutable in a courtroom, but she couldn't seem to manage that with Wyatt.

"Do you need to cry?"

"I don't want to," she said thickly.

"Let it out. I'm not scared of it, and if it helps, do it. You've been to hell and back, and all in a short time."

Her voice remained thick. "I haven't been to hell. People have worse than this happen to them." She speared a cherry tomato and popped it into her mouth, forcing herself to chew.

"Hell is relative," he said. "I like to say people have troubles, and it's kind of pointless to argue which is heavier, fifty pounds of rocks or fifty pounds of sand. Sure we could find someone who has it worse, but you've been lied to and betrayed, you had to give up your job and with it a chunk of the future you had planned, and you're unexpectedly on your way to becoming a mother. If none of that feels particularly good right now, I sure won't blame you. Big, little, who's to say. Fact is, your plate is full."

"I should be happy about the baby."

"Eventually."

She dared to look at him finally. "You don't think I'm awful?"

"No. Give yourself time. You've had a lot of shocks."

"You're kind," she murmured.

"Just honest."

She shook her head. "I'm so used to being in control, Wyatt. And I'm ashamed that when things went out of my control I couldn't handle it. I'm still not handling it. I seem to be on some kind of emotional roller coaster with no idea where I'm going, no idea why this is happening, no idea what to do about it. I don't like being helpless!"

He pushed a plate her way. "Hummus and crackers.

Unless I'm mistaken, carbs are good for your stomach right now. Don't just rely on salad. You might feel sick again. And you're far from helpless."

She swallowed hard, then decided he was right. Inviting as the salad had looked to her, the tomato didn't seem to be settling well. She reached for a cracker and spread some hummus on it. "How can you say I'm far from helpless? I've landed here and I'm taking advantage of your generosity. That's a long way from independent."

"You're not taking advantage of me at all. As for independence… Amber, none of us is truly independent. Sooner or later we need someone's help. How very nice it is to have friends. Life would be awful without them."

After dinner, he told her to go take a nap, anywhere she felt comfortable. She didn't argue. Weariness was weighing her down the way numbness had before. It *was* a roller coaster.

She went upstairs and changed into comfortable yoga pants and an oversize sweatshirt. She thought about stretching out on the bed, but it felt so far away. From what she didn't know, but she didn't want the privacy of this room right now.

Heading back downstairs, she heard Wyatt cleaning up in the kitchen. Part of her wanted to join him, but she was just too tired. She wandered into the living room, outfitted with overstuffed furniture in burgundies and blues, a large room that looked like it might have emerged from the set of a period piece. Smiling faintly, she guessed no one had changed this room in a very long time. It was probably almost ready to be roped off like a display in a museum.

How odd, she thought as she curled up on the sofa beneath a knitted afghan. She never would have imagined Wyatt living in a place like this.

A throw pillow cradled her head and she closed her eyes. Set free, her mind started to wander. What if she hadn't become pregnant?

Well, she wouldn't be here, that was for sure. She'd still be at the firm, ignoring the occasional stares until everyone else became bored.

But as sleep crept up on her, she decided she was very glad she was here. She felt comfortable with Wyatt. Felt as if she mattered.

And she wished he were holding her right now.

When she awoke, the only light in the room trickled in from the foyer beyond. Wyatt must have turned off the lamp in here.

She felt ever so much better, she realized as she sat up. As the throw tumbled from her shoulders, she discovered the room was a bit cool, despite what she was wearing. Wrapping the afghan around her, she rose and went to discover if it was the middle of the night or if Wyatt was still up.

Standing in the foyer, she at last picked out the sound of tapping keys from his office. From the kitchen, the refrigerator suddenly kicked on, humming. At night, in this big house, sounds seemed louder, more noticeable.

Well, she could head up to bed, but she wanted to be with Wyatt. She made her way down the hall to his office and found the door wide-open. He was intensely absorbed in reading on his computer, and as she looked she recognized the distinctive layout of an online law library.

After a moment's hesitation—because she didn't know if she should disturb him—she knocked lightly on the door frame.

Immediately he swung his chair around and smiled. "Feel better?"

"Much. Am I bothering you?"

He shook his head and motioned her to the armchair. "I was just catching up on my reading. Current federal Supreme Court filings. Some recent cases in this state."

"Trying to keep up can be almost a full-time job."

"Not unless you want to read every word. Mostly I just want to know what's out there so I can look it up when I need to." He gave a quiet laugh. "Then there are the times when I get intrigued and become too deeply involved in reading the facts of the cases."

"Some of them are fascinating."

"Some of them are head-scratchers. How many times have you asked yourself, *How in the heck did they manage to fall into this tangle?*"

"Truthfully? Rarely. Because I was mostly dealing with corporate clients, and their motivations were as clear as the contracts they weren't written in."

He laughed again, more heartily. "Remember Professor Jagger?" He lifted his voice to a higher tone. "'Most lawyers would be out of work if people were just honest.'"

Amber laughed with him. "So true. I certainly would have been, since I mostly dealt with contract disputes."

"Did you enjoy it?"

She thought about it. "I'm not sure," she said finally. "I didn't think about it, I just did my job. But sometimes…well, sometimes I'd get annoyed when I looked at deliberately fuzzy language and wondered how someone had gotten away with it. I mean, it's the job of people like me to make contracts clear, to avoid leaving wiggle room."

"So you came in on cases once the wiggle had showed up?"

"Sometimes. Then there were the contracts where the language was totally clear but expectations weren't." She shrugged. "Sometimes I had to remind myself that misunderstandings happen, and not all of them are malicious."

"Did you ever do estate law?"

"No. I hear when there's money involved, people can get really nasty, though."

He nodded. "So now you could move on to a different kind of law. Would you? You're as free as a bird to make a big change."

"Not quite free," she answered, her hand drifting toward her tummy. A baby. Little by little the child within her was becoming real, part of more and more of her thoughts. "Wyatt? Did you ever want kids?"

"I sure did. And do. I happen to like them. Especially before the world erases the wonder from them." His eyes crinkled at the corners. "Especially before they wind up explaining to me why they thought boosting a car for a joyride was a good idea, or why they couldn't resist drag racing down a public street."

She laughed again.

"You didn't eat much at dinner," he said, rising. "Let's get something in your tummy while you're feeling good."

Surprising her, he crossed to stand in front of her

and held out his hand. Gripping the throw with one hand, she reached out with her other and slipped it into his. At once she was overwhelmed by his warmth, the feeling of his skin against hers.

As they walked toward the kitchen, she realized she felt happy. Excited. Walking down the hall holding hands with this man made her feel good in a way she had seldom felt. Like her law school graduation day. Like when she got her first job with a big firm. Like the few times in her life when she'd felt her dreams were coming true.

"You seem to be feeling a whole lot better," he remarked.

"*Giddy* might be a better word." It was true, she thought as she entered the kitchen with him. Roller coaster indeed. Let the giddiness reign. It was like being on a first date with a guy she'd been crazy about forever, and she didn't want to quell the emotion.

"Why?" he asked.

She glanced at him in the bright overhead light, and all of a sudden the air went out of the room. He had a smile on his face, but his dark eyes seemed to reflect fire. Her heart skipped beats, and longing poured through her, happiness giving way to an almost painful hope and anticipation.

His voice became quiet. "Don't look at me like that. I might not be able to resist. Anyway, you need to eat something."

She fought to draw a breath. "No," she whispered. "Not now."

"What not now?"

"No food. Just you."

"God, Amber," he muttered. Then he lifted his hand

to cup her cheek, to run his thumb over her cheek-bone. "You're driving me crazy. I'm not supposed to feel like this."

"Why not?" she murmured, her whole body coming alive.

"Because you're in my care."

"To heck with that. Wyatt... I always wanted..."

He didn't let her speak another word. Bending his head, he brushed his lips lightly against hers, as if testing. At first she felt as if she were melting, a calm warmth flooding her. Then a quiver ran through her, and flames leaped along her nerve endings. All from that simple, tentative touch. She let the throw slide to the floor as her body heated.

Then his mouth brushed hers again. A soft moan escaped her and he returned for a deeper kiss, one that took possession of her mouth the way she wanted him to take possession of her entire body.

Yes, she'd wanted this all the way back when she'd been fresh to law school and he'd decided to help her along. All the time he'd avoided becoming more than her friend. All the time she had never dated the men closer to her age because Wyatt was all she wanted.

Time had passed, they were both different people, but the hunger in her had apparently never died. She had to know. Even if only once, she needed Wyatt's loving. It was a question that had been begging for an answer for more than a decade.

Her limbs began to turn syrupy. As if he sensed it, he slid an arm around her waist, but even as she reached up for more of his embrace, he broke the kiss gently and stepped back, holding her loosely.

"Wyatt?" she breathed.

"Not now," he answered. "Not now."

She opened her eyes and could have sworn she saw her desire reflected on his face, in his now heavily lidded eyes.

"You're vulnerable," he said simply. "Too vulnerable. So…"

So. She got it. She understood it, even. But that didn't mean she liked it. Somehow she was seated at the table and he was placing food in front of her, as if that would answer any of her cravings.

"It would be nice," she said eventually, "if you would tell me what just happened."

"You know," he answered. "We kissed. It's early days and you aren't in any way settled. I don't want you to ever feel I took advantage of you."

He was right and she knew it. She had admitted that she was riding a roller coaster right now. But understanding didn't diminish her huge disappointment. Saddened, she picked up the throw and draped it over the back of a chair.

Wyatt laid out leftovers that he thought might appeal to her, judging by her choices at other meals. She didn't seem inclined toward anything spicy, so he put out the potato salad, a couple of rolls that hadn't had time to go stale and some jelly and butter.

She reached immediately for a roll and spread it lightly with butter.

He could read the disappointment on her face, and he definitely shared it. He'd known a powerful moment when he'd kissed her, a need that had roared to life with an intensity that had taken him by surprise. Yeah, he knew he was attracted to her, knew he had to keep pushing aside sexual thoughts about her, but he'd kissed other women without responding that fast and hard.

Wow.

So yes, he was disappointed, too. But she wasn't through the worst of her reaction to all that had happened, as had been evidenced by the way her moods were swinging. He didn't want to make love to her in a moment of weakness only to add to her problems. Nor would he like himself very much if he did.

She ate half the roll and drank some milk. Pushing her plate aside, she said, "I'll settle down."

"I know you will," he answered.

She looked up and gave him an impish smile he hadn't seen since law school. "Then?"

"Then we'll see if we both still feel the same way."

"Good. Because I realized it hasn't changed in a decade."

His brows lifted.

"Really, Wyatt, did you think I was immune to you all those years ago? But despite what your father said about you being sweet on me back then, the off-limits signs were easy to read, even for me."

He studied her a moment, then laughed. "They were up to protect you."

"You've got to stop feeling like you have to protect everyone," she said. "Maybe I was too young ten years ago, I don't know. But I'm not too young now. Did you *really* want me back then?"

"Do you think I was a robot? Of course I wanted you. But you seemed like such a lost lamb at first, and I was so much older. I would have been a cradle robber."

"Not quite." She drew a long breath. "Just grant me one thing."

"What's that?"

"Admit that messed up or not, I'm an adult now. I'm entitled to my mistakes. God knows, I've made enough of them. Sheltering me doesn't protect me, it only leaves me more vulnerable because I lack experience."

"Meaning?"

"Meaning I might have had the sense to realize that Tom could have been lying. It's such an old lie, a man saying he's in the process of a divorce. Meaning that I should have had the experience to know that someone who could only meet me at lunch hour was probably leading me on and hiding me. There should have been red flags waving over that entire situation. Now that it's happened, I won't be so trusting in future. I've learned a painful but necessary lesson."

He leaned back in his chair, studying her thoughtfully. "You're right. But I can't take credit for sheltering you except that year in law school. And frankly, Amber, you were wide-open to every wolf who sniffed around, but you were totally focused on your studies. I may have been posted off-limits in your view, but you were pretty much swamped in a desire to succeed."

Her gaze wavered, then dropped. "You're right," she admitted. "I noticed you, but I didn't notice anyone else. And with the way I'd been raised, and my parents practically breathing over my shoulder with their expectations, I didn't leave much room to learn about life. It wasn't much better once I started practicing. Those big firms consume your life, especially at the lower levels."

"Don't take all the blame on yourself, though. Plenty of women have been misled by unscrupulous men like Tom. However, I would never advise you to stop trusting people, because most people are trustworthy. Unfortunately, that leaves you open to the creeps."

She nodded. "But…well…as a lawyer you often get to see the darker side of human nature. I failed to extrapolate."

He couldn't argue with that, but given that she'd been mostly involved in contracts law, she'd gotten a different view than if she'd handled divorces, trusts and estates.

On the other hand, his experience with family law and all its ugliness hadn't kept him from falling into Ellie's clutches.

He snorted, drawing her attention back to him.

"What?" she asked.

"I don't think there's any armor or knowledge that can prevent any of us from being fools at times. I almost married Ellie. I look back and wonder how I could have been so blind. Or she so deceptive." He shrugged. "Life is one big, long lesson. All I want for you is to get your feet under you again."

She'd been in his house for four days. During that time he'd seen her moods swing wildly. Hardly surprising with all that she had to absorb. He didn't remember her emotions bouncing around like this, so he didn't think it was her usual state. No, this resulted from too many shocks too quickly.

"I'm very attracted to you," he told her. "I want to get to know you a whole lot better. But I also want to see you comfortable in your own skin again. Fair enough?"

She nodded slowly. "I'm trying to get there."

"Just a bit at a time," he said. "You've got a lot to deal with, and it's not all going away overnight."

Chapter Eight

Morning sickness kept Amber at home the next morning. Wyatt had family court, and she'd wanted to see him in action, but not even crackers would settle her stomach enough to make her feel safe about going out.

Regretfully, she watched him drive off, then ran to the bathroom again, fearing the crackers were about to be lost. She sat on the stool in the powder room while cold sweat beaded her brow and her stomach churned, but she held her food down and eventually felt well enough to head for the kitchen and think about eating a few more crackers.

By lunchtime, just before she expected to see Wyatt's return, the doorbell rang. He hadn't said anyone might be stopping by, but she hesitated only a moment before going to answer it. He might be expecting a delivery.

She opened the heavy door with its stained-glass inset to see two very drab-looking women standing there. She blinked, wondering if they'd stepped out of a black-and-white movie—there wasn't a hint of color about them, their hair drawn severely back under old-fashioned hats with net that covered the tops of their faces. Their coats were just as drab, gray wool, fully buttoned up. Their dresses reached well below their knees and their feet were shod in sensible black oxfords. They might have come from another era.

"May I help you?" she asked.

"We're here to help *you*," said the older of the two women, her face stern.

"I'm sorry, but I don't need help."

"You do," said the older woman, stabbing her finger at Amber. "Living in sin with Judge Carter, not even married and carrying his child!"

"It's not his…" Amber began, her first impulse to protect Wyatt, even as a sense of unreality began to overtake her. Surely she had become unmoored in time.

"Lying, too," remarked the younger woman. "But it's not too late. Come with us. We'll help you find your way again."

Amber didn't care if she was rude. She closed the door in their faces.

What in the world?

Heavens, that had left her shaking. Unreal. Not like her to be so slow to react, but she soon forgot her nausea and trembling as anger replaced her initial reaction. Was that what they were saying about Wyatt around here?

She needed to leave. Now. He had that election coming up and if people were talking this way… The urge to run was almost overwhelming. She didn't want to harm Wyatt, no matter how unconcerned he'd seemed about it. Living in sin? She supposed some people still thought that way, but how many of them were around here, and how could that affect Wyatt?

He'd been kind enough to take her in, now she had to be kind enough to leave. It didn't matter where she went. The only thing that mattered was that she not mess up his life as well.

She had her foot on the bottom stair, prepared to pack and leave quickly, when she heard another knock on the door. If it was those women again, she was going to give them a piece of her mind. Her chin set with determination, the surprise that had kept her from responding before now gone, she marched back to the door and flung it open, ready to do battle.

It was Earl. "I see Wyatt's not home yet," he said cheerfully. "Mind if I come in, Amber?"

Her anger deflated instantly, and she felt her stomach roll over again. "Not at all." She tried to smile.

After he crossed the threshold and closed the door, he peered at her. "What's wrong?"

Like his son, he seemed to miss little.

"I had some visitors. They weren't very pleasant." She could talk to Earl, she realized. She knew he would be concerned about Wyatt's position as judge. He'd already offered to get out in front of rumors. Yes, she had to tell him.

"I didn't make coffee," she said frankly. "Too nauseated."

"I'm not surprised. My Beth had the morning sickness something bad. Well, come on, I can do with a beer as well as coffee."

He urged her into the kitchen and made her sit at the table. "Maybe not beer," he said, eyeing her face. "Might not smell good to you right now. Can you eat anything?"

"I was considering more crackers."

So Earl brought her the box of crackers and a plate and started a pot of coffee going. She liked him, just as she liked his son.

"So tell me about it," he said as he joined her at the table. "It must have upset you."

"Mostly for Wyatt's sake. These two women in very drab clothes..."

"Say no more," Earl interrupted. "I know them. I know the whole lot of them. Followers of Fred Loftis, who unfortunately owns our only pharmacy or I suspect he and his would have been ridden out of town a long while ago. Anyway, you don't need to worry about them. I'll see that they don't bother you again."

"I'm not worried about *me*," she said vehemently. "It was what they implied. I don't want to cost Wyatt his retention."

Earl sighed, rose and went to get a cup of coffee for himself. "Are you thirsty?"

"Water, please."

He brought both drinks to the table. "Wyatt told you he's not worried, right?"

"Of course. But should he be?"

Earl smiled. "Not about that lot. Judgmental bunch, and hardly anyone can stand them. You might give old Loftis an excuse to spout fire and brimstone for a few Sundays. And if you need anything from the pharmacy, send me to get it, because old Fred's not famous for keeping his yap shut. But put them out of your mind."

Wyatt walked in just then. As usual, he'd worn jeans and a gray sweater to court. Amber was surprised she hadn't heard him enter the house. "Put who out of her mind?" he asked.

"A couple of Loftis's women showed up here and upset Amber. I'll deal with them. They won't come round again."

Wyatt's face darkened. "They'd better not, or they'll be dealing with me."

"Trespass," Earl said. "I'll warn 'em. Then I might even enjoy watching you have them arrested."

At that the cloud passed from Wyatt's face and he laughed. "That would be a pleasure." He joined them at the table with a mug of coffee and reached out to lay his hand over Amber's. "I'm sorry I wasn't here to take care of them for you."

"I'm not worried about me," she said again. "But if people are talking about you like that…"

He shook his head. "People might be curious, but most of them won't take that tack about you visiting me."

Earl sniffed.

Amber looked at him.

Wyatt said, "Let's not do that again, Dad."

"Do what again?" Amber demanded.

Earl looked a little sheepish. "Well, before you got here I was telling Wyatt it wasn't a great idea right before the election. People *will* talk."

"See," said Amber, jumping in before Wyatt could

respond, "I've got to leave. If I'd known you had this election coming up I'd have gone somewhere else."

Both men spoke simultaneously. "No."

She blinked. "No what?"

"You're not leaving." Again they both spoke, sounding like a chorus.

She wrapped her hands around the glass of water she'd barely tasted and looked from one to the other, trying to figure this out. "Okay," she said finally. "I get that this never concerned Wyatt, but why did you change *your* mind, Earl?"

"Because I was wrong to be concerned. I told you when we had dinner, I think it's better if you stay. And I'm right. I've been poking my nose around since you arrived, and most people think it's nice that Wyatt has a friend visiting. Almost nobody seems inclined to criticize him for it."

"But if those women…"

"Those women won't be listened to by anyone outside their poisonous little group." Earl shrugged. "And, as usual, most people just don't give a damn one way or the other. Might make a nice topic of conversation for a few minutes, but… Wyatt was right. It's just not a big deal."

"Told you," Wyatt said.

After all the tension she'd been feeling, she almost giggled at the smug way Wyatt said that to his father. Earl grinned at him.

"In fact," Earl said, "the whole seven-day-wonder aspect of this may already be wearing off. Ellie, though…" Earl shook his head. "She can't make up her mind which story to try to spread. After what she said a year ago when she and Wyatt broke up, there's not a whole lot she can say about you being pregnant by him. This is fun to watch."

"Just as long as those women don't come back to bother Amber, I'm fine with it."

Glancing at him, Amber thought she wouldn't want to have to deal with an angry Judge Wyatt Carter.

"Bah," said Earl. "Now look, Amber, I know you don't have a license in this state, but I sure could use a little help at my office. You can practice under my license, help with motions, research and so on. Say, Monday afternoon?"

Wyatt snorted. "I should have known you had an ulterior motive."

"What ulterior motive? I can use help, and this lovely lady is hardly going to be happy rattling around in this big old house all by herself while you're in court."

Amber didn't even have to think about it. "I'd enjoy that, Earl."

Wyatt smiled. At first she couldn't imagine why, then she realized—she had just committed to staying. At least for a while.

Oh, boy. She hoped she hadn't made a bad decision.

That evening after a dinner of Wyatt's homemade chicken soup, he suggested they take that walk the doctor had recommended. Amber liked the idea. Now that her stomach had settled, she wanted some activity. She'd been here for five days now, and all she'd seen were a couple of pretty streets, the courthouse and a diner.

Donning jackets, they stepped out into the cooling night. The last signs of twilight were fading over the western mountains and the streetlights cast golden puddles of light on the sidewalks and streets. The air smelled amazingly fresh. She could even detect sage on the gentle breeze.

"I should really show you around my town," Wyatt remarked, tucking her arm through his. "You haven't seen much of the good that keeps me here. A morning in court, a visit to a doctor and two women hell-bent on salvation..."

She giggled. "Do you realize how that sounds? 'Hell-bent on salvation'?"

He laughed quietly. "I meant it exactly the way it sounds. Most of the time that group is just a minor irritant around the fringes. People hardly pay them any mind. We may like our gossip around here, but few people are cruel about it. Anyway, our city police chief, Jake Madison, is married to Loftis's daughter, Nora. That got a little attention. And then one of Loftis's followers tried to poison some of the chief's cattle as an expression of his displeasure, so for a while they had everyone's attention. Then things settled down again."

The streets were quiet, inviting. Lights glowed from the houses, giving Amber a few twinges of loneliness. So much life behind those windows, maybe a whole lot of love, and she'd never felt more on the outside in her life, not even as a too-young student in college and law school.

"There's the library," he said, pointing to the instantly recognizable facade of a Carnegie library. "Emmaline Dalton, the sheriff's wife, has been the librarian there since she left college. Her dad was a judge, too. Anyway, if you hear anyone mention Miss

Emma, they're talking about her. No one knows when it started, but that's what everyone always calls her."

"Miss Emma. I like the sound of it."

"You'd like her, too. And the sheriff, Gage Dalton. Now there was an interesting story."

"Yes?" Her curiosity piqued.

"Back when he first arrived here, Gage was a loner, a complete unknown. All anyone knew was his face was scarred from burns, he had a wicked limp and he lived above Mahoney's Bar. Every night he'd walk into the bar, have a shot, then take a long, painful walk. People started calling him Hell's Own Archangel."

"Really? Wow. He must have looked awful."

"A little scary, too. Anyway, he eventually took a room with Miss Emma…she was running a boarding-house mostly for women. I never heard the details of why she rented a room to Gage. Anyway, it was just after I left for college, so I don't know much about it, but I heard he wound up saving her life. Then marriage followed."

"And Gage? What had happened to him?"

"He used to work for the DEA. A car bomb killed his family and he barely survived."

Amber thought about that as they continued to stroll. "I guess he would have looked like Hell's Archangel after that."

"That would be my guess. Things have changed for him since Emma, though. Anyway, he went to work for our old sheriff Nate Tate… I hope you get to meet him. An icon in this town. When Nate retired, Gage was elected to replace him."

Amber could almost feel the threads that knit this town together. She envied the people who lived here.

They had something she'd never had—a community and lifelong friends. All the while she'd been pursuing her parents' goals and then her own, it seemed she had missed a huge chunk of life.

"You're lucky," she blurted.

"Me? Why?"

"Because you live in a place like this. Oh, I get it isn't perfect. I met some of the imperfection this afternoon, but…you must know so many people, have so many friends, it's… Well, I've never known anything like this."

"It's not Currier and Ives," he warned her. "Plenty of warts to share around."

"I'm sure." She sighed. "I guess I'm feeling…adrift. And like I missed something important."

He didn't answer as they continued down the block and rounded a corner onto another tree-lined street. Here the wind had ripped most of the autumn leaves from the branches. Bare fingers stretching upward and outward. She refused to consider them skeletal.

"Must be awfully pretty in the spring when the trees leaf out," she remarked.

"You're welcome to stay and see."

"Wyatt! I can't put you out like that."

"Who says you'd be putting me out?" he answered quietly. "I like coming home to see you. I hated how empty that house was before. Anyway, where will you go? To your father?"

"Oh, God, no."

"A friend?"

She fell silent. When she'd needed a friend, whom had she called?

"I thought so. You can stay with me. I'm not being

a male chauvinist when I say a woman shouldn't have to face pregnancy, birth and a newborn without some emotional support."

Actually, the thought of facing all that alone had terrified her when she allowed herself to think about it. She was a strong woman, able to take care of herself in the man's world of the law, but this?

"Women all over the world have a community of support," he continued. "You could have one here."

She glanced at the lamp-lit houses again and wondered if he could be right. If just a piece of that could be hers.

"Amber?"

She turned her head toward him, trying to drag herself out of the wisps of dreams that were probably unattainable for her. "Yes?"

"Remember what you said about having a pretend engagement?"

She almost flushed. "And you went all moral on me."

"Well, I'm not much fond of pretense. But it just occurred to me…you're about to have a baby without a father. Don't kids need fathers? If you married me, we could get you through this and I could help take care of the child in any way you think best."

She froze in her tracks and faced him. "What about pretense?" she demanded even as shock flooded her all the way to her toes. She was going hot and cold faster than she could believe.

"You suggested an engagement to end after the election." He faced her, too. "Amber, there's no pretense in a marriage. It's real."

Her jaw dropped. Words almost deserted her. Her

heart hammered wildly. She had no idea how long it was before she could speak. "Have you lost your mind?"

"Maybe," he answered. "It just popped into my head. Not like it's something I've been thinking about. But now that it popped out…well, I could take care of you and the child. So think about it."

Think about it? With difficulty she turned and started walking again, but this was no gentle stroll. She strode quickly, and when he took her arm again, he kept pace with her. A marriage? All because she was having a baby?

God help her, it sounded like a solution to all her fears and worries. Which, she supposed, made her despicable.

Wyatt deserved better. Much better.

They didn't speak again until they were back inside the house. Wyatt was still trying to figure out what had caused him to blurt that without thinking it through beforehand. He wasn't usually the type. He was also worried about the apparent shock he'd given Amber. Damn, what had he been thinking? Even if he wanted to ride to the rescue, there ought to be some easing into a question like that. But no matter how badly he had brought the subject up, it was out there and he wasn't backing down. He'd be lying if he told himself the possibility hadn't crossed his mind more than once over the years. A fantasy, just a fantasy, but now it somehow felt *right*.

He urged her into the kitchen for a warm drink and suggested a few cookies. She merely nodded. Apparently she was still stunned. Maybe even working up to a good rage. She'd have every right. She'd offered a pretend engagement, he'd gotten on his high horse and embarrassed her, and now he was offering marriage out of the blue.

She must wonder if he'd gone mad. He was certainly wondering.

He settled her at the kitchen table with chocolate chip cookies and asked if she wanted her milk warmed. She simply shook her head.

Oh, man, next thing she'd be packing up to escape this insane asylum. First those women this afternoon, and now him. Really?

She drank half her milk while he downed a beer and waited for whatever was to come. Weirdly enough, he had no desire to withdraw his proposal, even though her reaction told him the thought had never entered *her* mind, unlike his. But the attraction he felt was strong enough that he was sure it could grow. Whether it became love, who could tell right now? He just knew he needed to protect this woman and her child in any way he could.

"You know," she said finally, "the other day you didn't want us to make love because I needed time to settle."

He almost winced, because it was true.

"Now all of a sudden I'm settled enough to decide whether to marry you?"

She had a point. When she started drumming her fingers on the tabletop, he braced himself.

"Wyatt, you're not a knight-errant. You can't go around acting like Don Quixote and expect any better outcome than he had. Maybe this seems like a perfect solution for my problems to you. I admit, it's attractive to me. But marriage? That's a hell of a commitment for both of us when I'm just in a spot of trouble. A temporary spot of trouble."

One thing he had to say. "A child isn't temporary, Amber."

"You think I don't know that?" Her voice rose a little. "I've been spending the last month trying not to think about how *un*temporary this is. How to deal with it. How to change my entire future to accommodate it. I've spent more time denying my pregnancy than planning for it."

He nodded, not wanting to interrupt her.

"You've already hinted that I'm not of sound mind right now. Well, what about you? What the hell are you thinking?"

He took a moment, closing his eyes and searching deep within himself. He rarely blurted things. Being a lawyer and a judge had taught him to be very considered in all he did and said.

But thinking back to when he'd first known Amber, he faced something else, something she needed to know, even if it was uncomfortable for him. He opened his eyes and looked at her, glad to see her color was returning. For a little while there she had appeared pale.

"Wyatt?" she asked.

"You know, back when we were in law school, I was really attracted to you. My dad and I both told you that. But I was eight years older, and you seemed like a lost lamb. No way was I going to take advantage of you. But if you'd been older, I'd have asked you out. And if we hadn't been headed in different directions—me to the navy and you to the big law firms—we might be married right now."

Her eyes had widened, and she drew several quick breaths. "What are you saying?"

"I'm just saying that we've been friends for a long time. That if things had been different back then, we might have become more than friends. Honestly, I've even thought about it more than once. But now we're here."

"And once again you want to protect me," she said sharply.

"No," he said levelly. "I want to take care of you and this child. There's a difference. Anyway, marriage would guarantee that you'd be cared for even if something happened to me. You and the child. Who else am I going to take care of, Amber?"

Her face changed and he wished he could read what had suddenly made it so soft and sad all at once. "Just think about it," he said. "Like I said, marriage is real. This would be no pretense. You can tell me in the morning. If you say no, I'll never mention it again. And now you know the last of my secrets. I've always hankered after you."

Then he rose. "I need to go do some work. Come get me if you need anything."

The walk to his office, his ears straining to hear her call his name, seemed a lot longer than usual.

But she never called his name.

Amber ate a cookie absently, hardly tasting it, sipping some milk to wash it down. What in the world had possessed Wyatt? He said he wasn't concerned about the election. Maybe those women earlier today? Maybe he felt he needed to protect her from any more of that kind of attention? But wasn't marriage an extreme solution?

Then she remembered what he'd said: marriage was real, not a pretense. That he wanted to care for her and her child. That he'd sometimes thought about it in the past. So he meant it. But why?

Sure, she'd been attracted to him in law school. She'd had no idea back then that he reciprocated. None. He was always a perfect gentleman with her. Of all the men in law school, he was the last one she would have thought felt any sexual interest in her.

Had it lingered over the years? Apparently. When he'd kissed her, he'd said he'd wanted her all those years ago. So maybe having her back in his life—and not just at the other end of a phone call or email—had awakened those feelings again. They'd certainly preserved their friendship. Why not the rest of it, especially since it had never been expressed?

But marriage. That was such a huge commitment. He said he liked finding her here when he came home. He'd said something else, too, and it had tugged at her heartstrings: *Who else am I going to take care of?*

There was such loneliness in those words. Reaching for another cookie, she bit off a small piece, trying to focus on just that one thing. Wyatt was thirty-seven, maybe thirty-eight now. That was young in this day and age. But maybe he was longing for a family to fill this house, and maybe after Ellie he'd felt too burned to start over again with another woman. Or maybe there weren't a lot of prospects around here.

Regardless, the loneliness of those words reached through all her preoccupation and touched a part of her she'd thought would remain frozen forever. After

Tom, she'd told herself she wanted nothing to do with a man ever again. They were liars and cheats.

And then there was Wyatt, in a class by himself. He'd *always* been in a class by himself. Unfailingly honest and upright. If Wyatt said he'd do something, you could count on it. If he made a promise, he kept it. All these years he'd been a sort of touchstone for her, keeping her straight when the twisting paths of the law might have led her to take some turns that, while not illegal, would have made her ashamed later. And how many cases had he helped her think through over the years?

A good sounding board, a good friend and now... while he said he wanted to do something for her, she felt he needed something *from* her.

Rising, she walked down the hall to his office. The door was open. He turned at once from the papers in front of him. "Yes?"

"Tell me all about Ellie, Wyatt." Picking up the beautiful shawl he'd lent her, she seated herself on the comfortable chair and wrapped the delicate tatting around herself.

His brow furrowed. "Why? She's in the past."

But Amber thought she was very much in the present. That woman had wounded him deeply. Maybe as deeply or more deeply than Tom had wounded her. Certainly deeply enough that he was considering marriage to her. It wasn't the same as asking a total stranger to marry him, but the years had still flowed down the stream with the two of them apart, and did emails and phone calls make up for face time?

"I loved her," he finally said. "Or at least I loved

the woman I thought she was. Who can tell the difference? But it's over."

"Except that she's evidently still mad at you, according to your friend Hope. Maybe it's not over."

"It is for me," he said flatly. A spark appeared in his eye. It seemed he didn't like being questioned as if he were on the stand. What judge would?

She could have laughed if she hadn't been so concerned about him. And herself, too, but right now he was at the center of her worries.

Then he said something that struck her deeply. "I can honestly say that I think I know you better than I ever knew Ellie. All the conversations over the years... I know your moral compass. I know a lot about what drives you. I think you know me as well. Marriage is always a risk, Amber. Nobody can honestly promise that the vows will last forever, that the love will last forever. I see it in my courtroom all the time. So love isn't the only reason to get married. In fact, there may be better reasons."

She had to admit that was a novel idea to her. At least he wasn't trying to persuade her that he was in love with her. She wouldn't have believed it. In lust? Oh, yeah, they both were. But that was a long way from love.

"Anyway," he said, "I'm not withdrawing my offer. It might benefit us both...or not. Think about it. I could have us married by noon tomorrow, we could have a long engagement or we could just continue as we are for as long as you need and want. Your decision."

Which did nothing at all to help her parse through what had happened. What had propelled him to this offer? She looked at him and realized he was studying her, almost drinking her in. She could see the hint of passion in his expression, and her own body responded to it. Maybe if they just answered that need, everything else would become clearer.

But she knew one thing for certain—she didn't want him to take her under his wing the way he had during law school. If they were to move forward in any direction, she had to be an equal.

Oh, God, this was all a mess. He was a natural caretaker. A natural knight on a white horse. She'd seen it before. But she wasn't some helpless miss who needed rescuing. Yes, she needed help at the moment, and he was providing it. But that wouldn't be forever.

But right now...hell, it sounded so good to her. And she knew it would help protect him from the ugly gossip. Oddly enough, she wanted to take up her lance in his cause as well. She wondered if he even guessed that.

She almost smiled. Two knights-errant, charging forward. Each wanting to help the other.

Maybe he was right. Maybe there were better reasons for marriage than love.

"Sorry," he said finally. "I told you just to think about it. I'm not trying to pressure you one way or the other."

"Assuming *arguendo*," she said, using a lawyer's familiar Latin term to indicate a hypothetical, "that we marry. You've told me what you'd like to give me in terms of security. But what exactly would you expect from the arrangement?" She hoped she sounded clinical, because she was feeling anything but. Marriage. While it terrified her, it also meant that they'd share a bed, something she'd wanted to do with him for a long time. An old desire that had been growing larger since her arrival, despite everything else.

He steepled his fingers beneath his chin and regarded her steadily. "I'm going on thirty-eight years old. I live in a small town where there aren't any marital prospects that have caught my attention. Ellie's been the only one, and that was a helluva mistake. Then there's you. I think we'd have a chance to build something that would last. And frankly, Amber, I'd really like to have a family. The older I get, the more I seem to want it. Not that I'm trying to pin you here. I mean, I get that you might want to go to a practice elsewhere, but that doesn't mean we couldn't still have time together, here or wherever. The point, I guess, is that I'm sick of a solitary existence, and you and I have been friends for such a long time…well, I'd like to keep you rather than lose you. Like I said, I've always wanted you. That hasn't changed. I'd like to give it a try."

She thought over what he was saying. Wyatt, ever logical and truthful. He'd admitted he was lonely. Her trip here had awakened feelings long left behind for both of them. Whether they were enough…

She knew one thing for certain, though. Desire was muddying these waters. They'd both think more clearly once they'd satisfied it.

Without another thought, she rose from the chair, dropped the shawl and went to sit in his lap, twining her arms around his neck.

"So, Wyatt," she said quietly, "make love to me now."

He didn't reject her, but wrapped his arms around

her, holding her close. Then, gazing into her eyes, he said, "Why? Why now?"

"Because the smoldering between us is getting in the way of rational thought. I want to be sure neither of us is considering this for the sake of sex."

He continued to study her face, as if he were looking deeply into her being. She felt her heart racing, her breaths coming rapidly, her body turning into warm honey. And through it all an almost painful hope and expectation. Like teetering on a cliff edge, not knowing if she'd fall or find solid ground, but ready to fly.

He leaned in, taking her mouth in the gentlest of kisses. She let her head tip back, begging for more as her heartbeat seemed to strengthen in every part of her. Her thighs instinctively clamped, trying to find the answers she didn't yet have.

Then, slowly, gently, he eased her off his lap. Disappointment crashed through her, and her eyes began to burn with unshed tears.

"I'm going to lock up the house," he said quietly. "My bedroom is at the far end of the hall from yours. If you still want this, meet me there."

Crashing disappointment transfigured into amazing exhilaration and nervous hope. Yes. Oh, yes. She turned and headed for her room, filled with anticipation.

Chapter Nine

Wyatt didn't move for several minutes. He closed his eyes and considered what he had done and what he was about to do. It had seemed like such a logical solution for both of them: both of them lonely, her in trouble, him lacking things he wanted, a marriage that could give them both what they needed, at least right now.

Love didn't guarantee a successful marriage. Nothing could. So marrying for other reasons wasn't necessarily any riskier.

He had feelings for her, he just didn't know what kind. Protective, yes. Friendship, yes. Love? Who knew? It seemed too soon.

Oh, hell, he thought, rising. She was right. Once they'd made love, things should become clearer one way or another. The smoke would turn into fire, then die down.

Maybe then they could both really decide what they needed, and not just what they wanted.

It was crazy, all right, but even Wyatt Carter sometimes did crazy things, like racing a motorcycle around windy mountain roads, like off-roading in his ATV a little too fast. Like going to Afghanistan with the JAG as an investigator, a task for which he'd been required to take quite a bit of field training. He'd volunteered for that one.

So for all he presented a staid facade, there was a bit of wildness in his nature, and he guessed it was exerting itself now.

Shaking his head, he checked the few doors and windows that might have been opened at some point, then headed up to his room, half hoping that Amber would be there, half dreading that she wouldn't.

It was as if a puzzle from long ago was about to be completed. Maybe all these years part of him had been waiting for this woman. Who the hell could tell now? But he also knew from experience how rarely reality lived up to the dream.

This could destroy everything they'd managed to keep over the years. One way or another, it was certainly going to answer a question they'd both apparently had for a very long time.

Amber wasn't in his room. He looked down the long hallway and saw her closed door. His insides squeezed with disappointment. He seemed to remember that *she* had been the one who had sat in his lap and asked for lovemaking.

Sighing, telling himself he was overreacting to what was probably a good bit of common sense on her part, he stripped and stepped into his large private shower, washing the day away with hot water.

Oh, hell. He'd been ham-fisted about everything. Where were the hearts and flowers? The dating? The romantic interludes that were supposed to lead up to this? God, his offer had been so *logical*. What woman wanted a marriage proposal that sounded more like a merger?

Then, when he should have swept her into his arms and made passionate love to her on the rug, on the sofa…he'd coolly collected himself, mentioned locking up and told her to come to him if she still wanted this.

Cold-blooded. Stupid. Trying to give her space to change her mind, but he doubted she wanted that space or she wouldn't have so boldly sat on his lap.

As he toweled off, he wished he could kick himself. Wyatt Carter hadn't always had the temperament of a judge. Yeah, he'd never been one to leap easily into the deep end about anything, but this? These were the actions of a cold fish. Was that what he'd become? Hiding behind walls of restraint and logic? Because he seemed to be hiding.

He hadn't been like this with Ellie. Had she really scarred him so deeply that he'd locked his heart away?

Damn, he needed to apologize to Amber. If she hadn't felt offended before, she was probably rapidly getting there.

With a towel wrapped around his waist, he stepped out of his bath into his bedroom, and the first thing he saw was Amber. She stood there in a yellow terry-cloth robe, her hands fisted in the pockets.

"Amber…"

"Wyatt…"

They both spoke at once.

She immediately fell silent. Her chin was up, but this woman who had spent years wending her way through tough law firms and tough cases looked very uncertain right now.

He cussed.

"Wyatt?" She blinked. Well, of course, he didn't swear often, and never *that* word.

"I'm sorry," he said. Then he crossed to her, tugged one of her hands out of her pocket and drew her to the edge of his bed. "Please sit."

She did, then he sat beside her, reclaiming her one available hand.

She waited, looking at him.

"I just realized I handled this all poorly," he told her. "I offered marriage like a contract, and when you wanted to make love I sent you on your way while talking about locking up the house. In the romance department I get a great big goose egg."

She shook her head a little. "I didn't ask for romance. At least I don't think I did."

"Well, you deserve it."

She astonished him then, her expression becoming almost ferocious. "I had enough romance for four months, even if it was only over lunch hour. Flowers, candies, fancy foods, the finest hotel and promises of a future. I was dazzled, all right. Look where it got me. All of that can be faked. I don't trust it. You were honest. You gave me an option and you didn't conceal it in roses. If you had, I wouldn't have believed you."

Surprise rocked him again.

"I'll bet," she said more quietly, "that Ellie made you feel the same way. I know you're capable of the romantic part. You could do it if you wanted. But it's all… I don't know. Not as real as what you said to me today, at any rate. You were honest. That allows me to be honest. Thank you."

He certainly hadn't expected this, but he admired it. "Somehow I should have handled this better," he said, repeating his earlier thought.

"But how?" she asked. "We're friends. We're honest. You don't need to woo me, and I don't need it. God, Wyatt, I have a crying need for honesty. Just honesty."

He could understand that. He rather needed it himself after Ellie. But still…

She went on. "Maybe our courtship has been happening over ten years. I don't know. But you did absolutely nothing wrong today, and I want you to understand that. Believe it. You offered me what seemed like a perfectly logical solution to the problems I'm facing, to the things you want in your life. What the devil could be wrong with that?"

Plenty, he thought. "You asked if I'd gone mad and called me Don Quixote," he reminded her.

She flushed a bit. "Well, if you were dashing to my rescue alone…yes. But if there's something you need in a marriage…well, then it might be mutually beneficial."

Again he had the feeling that this was too damn clinical. They were both being cold about something that shouldn't be cold. Except treating this as a problem to be solved seemed to be the only place either of them could go comfortably.

Sighing, feeling as if they needed to find a way to break through to real emotions, the places they had both locked away, he drew her down on the bed beside him and wrapped his arms around her. He felt good when she hugged him back. Raising his hand, he stroked her dark hair.

"You're beautiful. You always have been."

"I'm older, and sometimes it shows."

He smiled faintly. "Not to me. You've grown into a marvelous woman. Maybe I'm glad I waited all these years."

She caught her breath then smiled. "There's that romance."

"It's true," he said. "Some things are well worth waiting for. I've been waiting for you forever."

She wiggled a bit and brought her mouth to his, giving him a butterfly kiss. "Let go, Wyatt," she breathed, closing her eyes. "Let the passion out."

Now it felt right, he thought, then utterly gave up thinking as he loosened the belt of her robe and tossed his towel aside. As he pushed the terry cloth back from her body, he found she exceeded his dreams. One would never have guessed from the clothes she chose to wear just how perfect and generous her figure was. She concealed it well, and probably deliberately, for professional reasons.

But she proved to be a cornucopia of delights to explore. Bending over her to kiss her again, plunging his tongue into her mouth, he began to run his hand over her, from behind her ear, which made her shiver, then down over her smooth throat.

"Oh, Wyatt," she breathed, and to his delight he felt her hands begin to caress him.

Yes, the time was right. Then long-denied passion swamped him.

* * *

Amber felt a wild, demanding urge to strip away all the restraints from this man. She wanted to see the raw side of Wyatt Carter, not the judge, not the lawyer, not the mentor. She wanted the part of him he had cloaked so carefully over the years.

She never doubted it was there. She had occasionally caught flashes of it, quickly tamped. She ran her hands over his shoulders, reveling in his smooth skin and the surprising strength she felt there. This was not a man who spent all his time at a desk or on the bench. She could feel his muscles bunching as he leaned over her, pillaging her mouth with a hunger that amazed her and then swamped her.

So good, she thought hazily. No kiss had ever felt like this, no tongue had ever been so welcome inside her mouth. Then he pulled his mouth away, and a mewl of protest escaped her, only to be silenced as his lips and tongue trailed downward, following the line of her throat as shivers ran through her, then trailing lower toward her breast.

She caught her breath, but he held her suspended in anticipation as his tongue trailed slowly, deliciously over the mound, avoiding her nipples. Just when she thought she could bear no more, he found one engorged nipple. The brush of his tongue over it felt like a lash of fire, and the flames ran straight to her center, deepening the hungry ache there. She needed…had she ever felt such need?

Surprising her, he moved suddenly, turning her one way then the other as he yanked the robe from her. No gentleness there, and she wanted none. When she reached for him, he caught her hands and pinned them to her sides.

"You're mine tonight," he muttered.

His. Oh, yes…

His mouth trailed lower, running over each rib and lower to just above the thatch between her thighs. Then back up it trailed until it found her other breast. This time it was no lash of the tongue. He drew her deeply into his mouth, sucking on her with a power that was almost painful, a power that seemed to want to draw her all the way inside him. Helplessly, her hips rolled, but he ignored the silent plea.

Just when she thought she could bear no more, he moved his mouth again, brushing a kiss on her lips, then slipping slowly downward. He never released her hands, holding her prisoner to his wishes, holding her prisoner to his desires and her own needs.

In taking control from her, he left her feeling strangely free, like a soaring bird. All she could do was experience whatever he chose to give her.

She gasped when he flipped her over. He caught her hands over her head and began to sprinkle kisses over her back until he reached her bottom and kissed her there. The sensation was so exquisite, so new, so exciting that moans began to escape her.

He took liberties with her, teaching her new things about her body, and she loved every sensation. Then he released her hands, and just as she thought she was about to become an active participant, he lifted her hips and slid into her from behind. She cried out with pleasure as his erection stretched her, filled her, answered the need that seemed to have always been there. Then his hand slipped around in front and cupped her, his fingers spreading her and teasing that hypersensitive nub of nerves.

She felt utterly possessed, utterly beautiful, utterly wild as he pumped into her from behind and lifted her higher and higher until her entire body felt as taut as a bowstring.

She hardly heard her own moans, in thrall to the roaring waterfall of feelings that was sweeping her away into unknown territory.

And then, in an instant, she arched, almost hurting as the orgasm ripped through her from head to toe.

He didn't give her long. Didn't allow her to collapse. Before she felt the descent to peace, he'd rolled over, bringing her with him, lifting her until she straddled his hips.

"Ride me," he said hoarsely.

His hands gripped her hips, guiding her until he once again filled her. She threw her head back, thrilled, feeling the tension building in her all over again. His hands urged her on until the rhythm became perfect. The ache in her rose impossibly until she shattered in satisfaction.

And this time she felt him join her, felt the sheer delight of him jetting into her, pumping more strongly, then finally easing until he drew her down on his chest.

Amber couldn't move a muscle. She rested on Wyatt feeling as if the last strength had been drained from her, but also feeling more content than she ever had in her life.

She never wanted to move again. Never before had she felt what Wyatt had just made her feel. Never. She wished it never had to end.

But finally, as the perspiration on her body began to dry, she felt chilled. Almost as if he sensed it, Wyatt lifted her easily to the side of the bed. Then he sat up and tugged her gently until she followed him to the bathroom.

Once there, he turned on the water in the shower then held her close, saying nothing, his face in her hair while she buried hers in his shoulder. After a few minutes, he reached out to test the water, then drew her into the large cubicle with him, putting her right under the comfortably hot spray.

She opened her eyes and saw him smiling at her, an almost wistful smile. Without a word, he began to soap her from her shoulders to her feet. She spared a moment to be grateful the enclosure was so big, because she wouldn't have wanted to miss a single sensation.

Each silky sweep of his hands and the bar of soap seemed to refresh her and excite her anew. When he had done both sides of her, taking his time, he turned her to face him, and now his smile was wider. "Feel good?"

She took the bar of soap from him. "Let's see."

He was a magnificent man, she thought as she ran her hands all over him, admiring the strength of his arms and shoulders, the power of his chest, the narrowness of his hips. Feeling a bit wicked, she spent some extra time on his privates until finally his hands reached for her head.

"Witch," he said. "Stop."

She laughed and did as he asked. After all, there were still his perfectly formed legs. When he turned around to let her soap his back, she paused.

"Wyatt? This scar…"

"I was in Afghanistan for a while," he answered. "It wasn't the safest place on earth."

"You never said!"

"I wasn't allowed to."

The thought disturbed her, driving away the growing net that desire had been casting over her. He faced her immediately. "It's okay," he said, then pulled their slick bodies together for a deep kiss.

It was over. He rinsed them both and then stood her on the large mat while he briskly toweled her dry. He gave her an extra towel to wrap around her wet head and grabbed one to tuck at his waist.

"I'm sorry," she said.

"For what?"

"For breaking the mood. I shouldn't have said…"

He laid a finger over her lips. "You didn't do anything wrong. No apologies, please. We just spent some time in heaven. Unfortunately our feet have to hit the ground again."

She nodded, knowing he was right but hating it anyway. She wanted that heaven again, wanted to never let go of it, no matter how unreasonable she was being. Summoning a smile, she decided to keep that to herself.

She didn't want him to feel bad, not after what he had given her.

She wrapped herself in her bathrobe, and Wyatt donned his own, a rich burgundy color that suited him. Together they went downstairs.

"I have a theory we need to try," he said.

"Which is?"

"That maybe if you eat something before you go to bed the morning sickness won't be so bad."

"I'm willing." She balanced the towel that was still wrapped around her hair.

"That's going to make it hard to sleep tonight," he remarked as he saw the gesture.

"I *do* have a blow dryer," she said wryly.

"Then let me do it for you after we eat."

He pulled out the toaster, suggesting they stick with toast and jam. "Who knows when morning sickness starts, but we're getting close."

She looked toward the digital clock on the microwave, and surprise jolted her. "Where did the time go?"

"I think we were having a good time." He winked, enjoying it when she blushed faintly.

"A very good time," she agreed huskily. "The best time ever."

Man, did that make him feel good. He could identify with a conqueror of old. He busied himself making the toast, hating the interruption but hoping she'd feel better in the morning if she didn't wake with a completely empty stomach.

At last he was able to put a stack of toast and a selection of jams on the table, along with a glass of milk for her. Instead of sitting across from her, however, he sat right beside her.

Much as he'd wanted her all those years ago, he wanted her more now. He hoped to God he hadn't just made a big mistake that would hurt both of them.

Conversation had died away. Far from wanting to talk, it was as if the haze of desire was growing around them again, making speech difficult as thoughts ran along racier paths.

After he got a couple of pieces of toast into her, he guided her back upstairs. "Get your blow dryer," he said. "You'll sleep with me tonight?"

The expression on her face made his heart skip a couple of beats. "Of course," she answered softly.

Yeehaw, he thought. Better than racing around mountain curves at high speeds on his motorcycle. Better than anything.

She brought her crackers, too, and soon he had her sitting in the rocker near the bed, running her brush through her hair as he used the dryer. She'd never worn her hair long, so the job was easy. Soon her bob was sleek and smooth again.

"That was a treat," she said when he switched off the blow dryer. "Do you do this often?"

"I've never done it before for anyone."

He came around to stand in front of her, smiling and holding out both hands. "Sleep," he said. "You need it."

"If we can," she retorted, making him laugh.

Naked, they crawled under the covers together, and soon Wyatt was spooning Amber from behind. He would have made love to her again, as passion rebuilt in him throughout every cell, humming until he felt he was connected to an electrical circuit.

But it was late. The digital alarm clock warned him in red numbers, and the doctor had said she needed her rest. So he kissed her hair and the nape of her neck, murmuring, "Sleep, Amber. There's always tomorrow."

It was a promise he wondered if he would be able to keep.

* * *

Curled up with her back against Wyatt, Amber allowed the good feelings to flow. It seemed like almost forever since she had last felt anything approaching this happiness and contentment. Even during the first heady days with Tom, she was quite sure she had never felt like this.

Wyatt had satisfied her at levels Tom had never even tried to reach, and then afterward, instead of bundling her on her way, he had taken care of her needs, from a shower to food.

The years collapsed, and she remembered Wyatt as he had been in law school, extremely attractive, wonderfully confident and always helpful and kind. He'd been remarkable then, and from what she'd seen, the years had only made him more so.

He was blessed with a judicial temperament, and she wondered if the people here had any idea how fortunate they were to have him on the bench. She'd seen enough judges in her day to tell a good one from a bad one.

But as he'd shown her, he was also full of passion. Wyatt cutting loose was magnificent.

She smiled into the dark and wiggled backward a little to get closer to him.

"Keep that up and there won't be any sleep," he mumbled.

She smiled into the dark, but a heaviness began to fill her, too. She couldn't remain Wyatt's dependent forever, and while he had offered marriage, she was sure he hadn't thought it through. To be father to another man's child? Maybe he could. But it remained, she had to build a future for herself, and there didn't seem to be a whole lot of opportunity for lawyers around here.

She pushed the sad thoughts aside, however. There was always tomorrow, as he'd said. For now she just wanted to cherish the glow.

Chapter Ten

The instant she sat up in the morning, nausea washed over Amber.

"Oh, God," she said and flopped back down.

Wyatt was still beside her. He raised himself immediately on an elbow, looking down at her with concern. "I take it the toast last night didn't help."

She swallowed hard. "'Fraid not."

"Crackers?"

"Give me a minute."

It had been lying in wait for the moment she moved, she thought irritably. She'd opened her eyes, seen sunlight flooding through a crack in the curtains and she had smiled as memories of last night flooded her. Then, because she needed to answer the call of nature, she had sat up.

Morning sickness had pounced on her like a cat

on a mouse. Now she was afraid to move, but she still needed to get to the bathroom.

"Crap," she muttered.

"Conflicting needs?" he asked, as if he could read her mind.

"Yeah."

He rolled out of the other side of the bed and came to perch right beside her, reaching for the box of crackers. He passed her a single cracker. "Try this while I get you some water to wash it down."

It felt so wrong to be eating a cracker in bed. Crumbs. But Wyatt hurried into the bathroom to get water, and she obediently nibbled the dryness, hoping it would help. She didn't want to get sick all over his bedroom rug, but there was something even more embarrassing likely to happen if she didn't move soon.

He was back with the water before she had finished half the cracker and perched beside her again. "When you're ready, raise your head as far as you dare."

She shoved the remainder of the cracker into her mouth and chewed. It seemed to stick in her throat, so she lifted her head to sip water and immediately regretted it.

Her head flopped back on the pillow.

"Wyatt…"

"I get it. Hold on a sec."

He grabbed a wastebasket from the bathroom and returned waving it. "In case," he said cheerfully enough. "Now let's get you on your feet. Don't worry about a thing."

He helped her out of bed. Her stomach roiled so much that she hardly cared they were both naked as jaybirds. With his arm around her waist, the wastebasket in front of her, he guided her into the bathroom and helped her sit. He put the basket in front of her feet.

"I suppose," he said, "you'd like privacy for this."

"Yup," she said, forcing the word out.

He closed the door, leaving her alone with her misery. God, this was awful. Was it this bad for most women? How many more weeks...

But eventually she got the cracker all the way down, with the help of the water Wyatt had left on the edge of the sink. Even just that little bit helped enough to make it possible for her to stand.

Embarrassed by her own weakness, she eased back into the bedroom. Wyatt was waiting patiently, still standing. "Okay?" he asked.

"A little better."

"Then how about we get you wrapped up and downstairs for some dry toast or fresher crackers."

He helped her into her robe and slippers, then pulled on his own. This time he didn't hold her hand as they went downstairs but kept her arm tucked firmly through his as if he was afraid she might fall.

"I know I can't help it," she said, "but this is embarrassing anyway."

"Why? Apparently it's perfectly normal. I've even heard that it's a good sign. Regardless, this is the last thing that should embarrass you."

In the kitchen—which had a tile floor, thank goodness—she reviewed her own situation with something between irritation and amusement. It was bad only at the very first, she admitted. Once she got a little something in her stomach, it eased, not totally going away, but it eased enough for her to carry on. She supposed she should be grateful for that.

But the idea that she might feel like she had a borderline case of stomach virus for weeks didn't appeal to her.

"God," she said finally.

"What?" He was brewing coffee and making toast.

"This is disabling."

He turned to study her. "How so?"

"Well, while this is going on, I can hardly pop into my car and move on. I'm not sure I'd interview very well, as ill as I feel most of the day. I mean, it's not intolerable except for first thing, but I can't ignore it. I feel sick."

He brought some of the toast and coffee to the table. "Milk?"

"Not yet," she answered.

"Okay." He sat across from her. "First of all, you don't have to hit the road. I thought I'd made that clear. You'll get past this. Maybe it won't be this bad after a while. Regardless, just take it easy until you feel completely fit again. Then you can make your decisions."

Not that she was in a hurry to go anywhere. She looked at the dry toast and wondered if she could handle it. Especially since last night. But being dependent rankled. She'd never been dependent before.

She also noticed that Wyatt hadn't mentioned his proposal again. Was he just giving her space or regretting it? After last night, she'd hate to think he wished he'd never offered marriage. As shocking as it had originally seemed, after the lovemaking they'd shared, it didn't feel shocking at all. She wanted to play with the idea, think about it, imagine a future being married to him before she made up her mind.

But if he was no longer interested...

She sighed.

"Penny?" he said.

She put her chin in her hand, arguing with herself. If she brought up the proposal, he might feel stuck. If she didn't mention it, she might never know. Was it so important that she know? He could always bring it up again.

"Oh, heck," she said finally. "Your proposal. Would you like to withdraw it?"

"I thought I'd made it very clear last night. I don't leap into the sack with just anyone. The proposal stands. Why? Are you thinking about it?"

"Of course I'm thinking about it," she snapped. "How could I not think about it? It's like telling me to ignore the elephant in the room."

"Hmm," he said, then a twinkle came to his eyes. "The elephant? I like elephants, but I'd also like my proposal to be a bit more attractive than that."

"Oh, hush," she said.

"Besides, you're feeling pretty bad this morning. Not a time for thinking about much except getting through this."

Except she *was* thinking about more than her morning sickness. Last night still flooded her senses and her mind. This morning his proposal sounded almost irresistible. At the same time, she had to decide from a position of strength, not weakness. It wouldn't be fair to Wyatt to use him as a life preserver when she felt she was drowning.

"Amber? Just put it aside for now. My offer isn't going away, so take your time, decide what's best for you, okay?"

She nodded, but she was honestly beginning to

wonder what was best for her. She'd been pursuing one goal for so long, and last month when she'd resigned from the firm, she'd felt her life had been totally upended, her prospects now limited. Partly because she'd have a child, but partly because leaving a firm after six months, no matter how good a recommendation they'd give to make sure she didn't cause any trouble, still looked bad. Large law firms didn't want to hire someone who might leave so quickly. There was just too much to learn about clients, and most such firms expected a lawyer to remain for many years, if not for the rest of their lives.

She had made herself look flighty, and everyone she sent a résumé to would wonder what was wrong with her.

She'd been wrecked the whole time she'd packed up to leave. But always at the back of her mind, little as she'd wanted to think about it, was the child growing inside her. Ninety-hour weeks were now out of the question. Even if she could afford a nanny for all those hours, at some level it struck her as wrong. If she brought a child into this world, she owed it more than material support. Much more.

And some wistful little corner of her mind had been pressing her more and more with a desire to see the first steps, hear the first word, enjoy the first smile. Yes, working women had to turn to day care. She got it. But not for ninety or a hundred hours a week.

She bit into some dry toast and washed it down with water. It stayed down, although it didn't cure the remaining nausea. "So we're having a party tonight?"

"Not exactly. Just a few friends I thought you'd like to meet. I can cancel it if you want."

"Let me think about it. I'm not antisocial, it's just…" Just that she didn't want to sink any roots in this place. Not when she was at least half-sure she'd have to leave.

But she *had* enjoyed meeting Hope and Julie. It would be nice, if she were here a few more months, to know some people she might be able to pal around with occasionally. She certainly wasn't used to long, empty days, and Wyatt still needed to work.

"I'm not used to having nothing to do," she remarked.

"Me, either," he agreed. "Well, Dad has said you can work with him if you want. And you're welcome to come to court with me when you feel well enough. I'm sure there's more than enough work to go around. Too bad you don't have your Wyoming bar license. We could sure use a pro bono public defender around here."

It was a fact that while the Supreme Court had said all accused persons were entitled to a legal defense, most places underfunded public defenders compared to prosecutors.

"I don't know criminal law," she remarked.

"You could learn fast. Or you could get into family law. Regardless, you'd have to see about licensing. If you're still licensed in Missouri…"

"I am."

"Then Wyoming offers reciprocity."

She nodded. That would make things easier. Far easier. No miserable bar exam to repeat. "I'll think about it."

And she would. She hadn't been in Conard City for long, nor seen much of it, but she already liked it here. It struck her as a friendly place to live, a good environment to raise a child.

There she was again, thinking about her child. She guessed it was sinking in at last, perhaps made real by her morning sickness. About time, too. She wasn't an ostrich by nature, although recent events with Tom might leave that an open question.

She realized she'd eaten half a piece of toast and was feeling somewhat better. "Thanks for the toast. It's working."

Wyatt smiled. "Good news then."

"Do you need to work today?"

"No. I've still got some papers to review before Monday, but that won't take long. As for tonight, I ordered a bunch of deadly sins from the bakery, so all I'll need to do is make coffee and tea. In short, I'm all yours for the day. Is there something you want to do?"

"Walk around town," she said. "I'd like to get to know this place better."

Wyatt was agreeable, but he figured once she looked around and saw how little there really was here, she'd probably be checking out cities again. After all, her whole life had aimed that way. Now she was in a tiny town, which showed movies only on weekends and where the biggest entertainment was plays at the college or the county fair. Or dancing at one of the roadhouses, which could get a bit risky when the cowboys got frisky.

Yet, it was better she know exactly what she was looking at if she thought about staying here. He was sure the PD's office would keep her really busy, as would working part-time for his dad...or even getting her license and joining the Carter practice. But however accustomed Amber was to working around the clock seven days a week, a person needed more in her life. Here she'd have enough free time to look for other things, for herself and her child.

He hoped she wasn't horrified, because after last night he'd have offered her marriage all over again.

He'd have liked to offer her love as well, but he didn't think it was there. Not yet. And he was far too old to mistake passion for love.

"We can walk around this end of town when you're ready," he said. "Later I'll drive you a bit. It may be tiny, but if you want to see everything, we'll need wheels. Too bad I won't put you on my motorcycle in your condition."

He enjoyed watching her jaw drop and her eyes widen. "You have a motorcycle?"

"A big black hog. I'm dangerous on mountain roads."

Laughter escaped her, and finally she had to wipe her eyes. "Wyatt, you'll never cease to surprise me. I never would have imagined you with a motorcycle."

He wiggled his eyebrows. "I am not what I seem."

"Apparently not."

He enjoyed her laughter and the smiles that followed. It wasn't long before she felt well enough to go upstairs to shower and dress.

A good morning, he thought. He just hoped the town didn't disappoint her.

The midmorning air was a bit chilly, whispering of winter's approach. The trees were mostly bare, although here and there patches of autumn color remained. Only a block over from his house was a park, and since it was Saturday it was full of young children and their parents. Amber paused, smiling as she watched them. The parents knotted together on various benches, keeping one eye on their children while they chatted. She loved it.

New urges were stirring in her. She wanted to be one of those parents on the bench watching a small child and talking with friends.

Man, she'd never seen herself that way before, but she was seeing it now. When at last they turned away and walked down another pleasant street, she wondered at herself. Was this the result of changing hormones, or was she just facing that a lot had been missing from her life, and now she wanted it? How could she know?

Their talk was desultory. He told her stories about the town, about its past, about things he remembered and things he'd heard about. There was a time when someone had been dumping toxic chemicals in an arroyo on a ranch. The time a devil-worshipping cult had tried to make a sacrifice of Miss Emma. Other stories, each of them almost a warning that as peaceful as the place appeared, it wasn't always so. They'd had a serial killer, an arsonist…all the bad types of people who existed everywhere.

Yet still the town felt quietly and contentedly settled. Not even the economic hard times that came and went could break up families and friendships.

Amazing.

People nodded and smiled as they passed, some waving from their front porches. Front porches. She'd almost forgotten they existed. A few others out walking paused briefly to chat with Wyatt and to be introduced to Amber. Then they hurried on because it was

Saturday and they had errands. Catch-up day, Amber thought with amusement. True everywhere.

When they got back to the house, Wyatt insisted she eat something. It was easy now; the nausea had died down to almost nothing, so she joined him in a liverwurst sandwich.

After lunch he drove her out to the community college campus, a hive of activity, much of it occurring on sports fields. Then back through town with its small businesses, and a stop at the bakery to pick up the goodies for tonight.

"Next weekend," he said, "I'll take you up into the mountains, and maybe to a friend's ranch."

"I'd love that." Another week. The urge to move on was rapidly vanishing.

"When we get home," he said, "maybe you should consider a nap. I was warned to make sure you get your rest. You certainly got your walk."

Since Amber seemed strangely reluctant to go off by herself to nap, Wyatt took her upstairs with him. In a minute he'd smoothed the sheets and coverlet still rumpled from the night and encouraged her to lie down on top of the covers with him.

She'd be asleep soon, he thought, but in the meantime he was only too happy to hold her close, stroke her hair and back, and listen to her breathing slow and deep. She *was* tired, more tired than she had probably thought, but she didn't want to be by herself. Didn't want to leave him behind.

That tugged at his heart. This woman was essentially all alone in the world. He got it. It was probably meaningless that she was clinging to an old friend, but he liked it anyway. Liked knowing that the lovemaking they'd shared last night had only made her feel closer to him. There was no more reluctance on her part to reach out and touch him. She'd done it dozens of times today, just casual touches, but they hadn't been there before.

Inevitably, he wondered if he'd be able to keep her. And inevitably he realized he couldn't. As far as he knew, this was not the kind of life that Amber had ever wanted for herself. The baby, leaving her job… those were temporary hitches he was certain she was smart enough to deal with in a way that pleased her.

He didn't fit into that equation, although he was still surprised that she'd brought up his proposal. He'd expected her to act like it had never happened.

It had sounded so cold-blooded, so calculating. *Here's what you need, here's what I want, so let's make a deal.*

Damn, that got uglier the more he thought about it. Forget his intentions. He wasn't even sure he remembered what had moved him to make the offer. But what he knew now was that it hadn't been pretty.

It had been a moment of wildness on his part. He was prone to them from time to time and had spent a lot of his life learning to temper the impulse or direct those moments safely.

Now he'd done the wildest thing of all, and he disliked himself for it. Amber had enough on her plate without him leaping on to join the load.

But last night… He sighed and snuggled her closer, drawing a murmur from her even as she slept. All unconsciously she wound her arm around his waist. It felt so good he closed his eyes.

Maybe it was time to give some serious thought to

exactly what he was doing here. He'd been winging it since the moment she'd told him she was in trouble. His only thought had been to give her a place to stay while she sorted her life out.

Any friend would do that. But not just any friend would offer marriage, and certainly not the way he had. Not just any friend would take her into his bed and unleash a new craving, stronger than any he had ever felt before for her. Stronger than any he had ever felt in his life.

He'd messed up. Earl would be delighted if he knew. On the surface, at any rate, he thought Wyatt was too sedate and straitlaced. Needed to kick up his heels more. A funny attitude from a dad who was equally worried about his "judicial decorum." What did he expect Wyatt to do? Travel to another state and have a fling?

Which, thought Wyatt wryly, was probably what at least part of this town was already thinking he'd done.

A couple of hours later, noises from outside woke him from his doze. Wyatt eased carefully away from Amber, trying not to wake her, and went to look out the window with the street view.

Hell, it looked like Loftis's ladies were out in force. He was being picketed, by God. They waved hand-made signs with words like *Sinner* and *Abomination* on them. He decided that was enough.

He straightened himself quickly, running a brush through his hair, tucking his flannel shirt into his jeans and jamming his feet into his boots.

Time to deal with these jerks. He didn't want them

bothering Amber, and he had guests coming in a few hours.

On the way downstairs, he called the dispatcher for the sheriff's office and police department. In this town they were one and the same.

He got Velma, old as the hills, and her ragged smoker's voice. "Velma, Wyatt Carter. I'm being picketed by some of Loftis's people."

Velma snorted. "Probably no law against it, but Jake and Gage will find a way."

"Or I will," Wyatt said. He was, after all, a judge. And while sidewalks were public property, his lawn wasn't. However, being a judge, he knew the limits of what he could do, and as much as he'd like to erupt at these women, he figured he'd only make it worse. Time for some of that damn judicial restraint, despite his annoyance.

"You hang on, honey," Velma said. "I'm rousing the troops."

He wondered what troops she meant. A deputy or two?

As soon as he stepped out on the front porch, the picket line of maybe ten women grew louder, shouting various ugly condemnations his way. He was a sinner, an abomination and some other things he didn't bother to really hear. He went to the edge of his porch and stood, folding his arms, simply staring at them.

Presently, their shouts began to trail off as his continued silence and inaction began to make them uneasy. When they became quieter—although not completely quiet—he raised his voice to be heard.

"Ladies, while you're free to protest on the public sidewalk, it's incumbent on me to warn you that you are disturbing the peace. You can be arrested for that. I suggest you protest quietly, especially since this is a residential neighborhood."

Well, that didn't work. Now he heard shouts of how he was violating their constitutional rights. It was all he could do not to grin. Most people didn't realize that there were time, place and manner restrictions on the First Amendment, allowed by the Supreme Court. They'd have done better to protest in the courthouse square.

Some of his neighbors had come out on their porches and waved to him. He didn't wave back. He wasn't going to do a thing to encourage these women. All he could see was that this might convince Amber to move on, and he didn't want that.

So he stood, keeping his arms folded, and simply stared. He didn't want to provoke trouble, but he was going to make it absolutely clear that they didn't intimidate him in the least.

Then the sound of approaching engines and flashing lights caught his attention. He looked to his left and saw a sheriff's cruiser, flanked by a city police car, coming down the street. Between them they blocked all traffic.

Then, to his utter amazement, he saw a small crowd behind them. *What the...?* When Velma had said she was going to call out the troops, he hadn't expected a counterdemonstration. Now he almost wanted to laugh.

The two police cars came to a halt just before they reached the line of women on his sidewalk, and Sheriff Gage Dalton and Police Chief Jake Madison climbed out.

"Howdy, Judge," Gage called. "Just here to ensure everything remains peaceable."

"Thanks, Sheriff."

Then from the other direction came two more cars, county and city. A whole section of street was now effectively blocked.

And into that section of street poured the crowd that had followed Jake and Gage in. Oh, this was priceless, Wyatt thought, trying not to grin. Outnumbered by the dozens of people on the street, the women on the sidewalk began to look uncertain.

Wyatt came down from the porch while a few voices from the street told the women to go home. One elderly man, leaning on a cane, spoke angrily. "You women go home and mind your own business, not everybody else's!"

Smothering a laugh, Wyatt ignored him and walked up to the women on the sidewalk.

"Ladies," he said, "you really should go home. Even though the sheriff and the chief are here to keep you safe, with this many people around, there could be a slip, which might cause trouble. Consider your message received."

"What are you going to do about it?" demanded one of the women, her gaze fiery.

"The right thing," he said, then stared her down.

"You'd better watch your step," she spat.

Gage Dalton, only a few feet away, asked mildly, "Was that a threat?" The woman clamped her mouth tightly shut.

"I don't feel threatened," Wyatt said easily. "These ladies are just doing what they think is right. But let me make something perfectly clear," he said, raising his voice a bit. "Do not trespass on my property or harass my guests. I *will* file charges. You've been warned."

Looking at once afraid and furious, the women stormed off down the sidewalk and around the corner to wherever they'd come from.

The crowd in the middle of the street clapped and whistled, and Wyatt walked out among them to thank them. He knew all of them to one degree or another, and he shook a lot of hands and received a lot of claps to his shoulders.

God, it felt good. Dozens of people had dropped everything to come help him out. His love for his community nearly overwhelmed him.

Wanting to thank them, he invited them in and broke out the treats he'd picked up at the bakery. So much for his small gathering tonight, but he knew his friends would understand.

Then, after he started the coffee and teakettle, he ran upstairs to check on Amber. She was standing at the window in his bedroom, and when she turned there was a smile on her face.

"Quite some show, Judge."

"I had a lot of help from my friends."

"I saw. I heard you, too. You were quite restrained under the circumstances."

He shook his head. "I didn't want to be. I don't want those biddies bugging you at all. But I couldn't see any point in making it any worse."

She walked toward him, right into his arms. Their lips met in a kiss he never wanted to end, but after a minute she pulled back a bit. "I hear a party downstairs, and as much as I want to tumble in bed with you…"

"It would be rude of me." He gave her a squeeze, cupping her rump to lift her up against him briefly, and dropped another kiss on her lips. "Come down if you want to. They're great people."

"I actually saw that." Her smile was wide.

God, he hated to leave her, but there was no escaping the fact that he'd just opened his house and he had no doubt the crowd was going to grow. His neighbors, then others who heard about it. Dang, he should have made a ton of chili anyway.

As it happened, a potluck was soon taking place. It filled his front porch and yard and spilled into the backyard, where there were tables and chairs. Soon there was even music.

He paused by Gage, who was eating a sandwich someone had brought. "And to think I warned those women about disturbing the peace."

Gage laughed. "This is a different kind of disturbance. All your neighbors are here."

And then some, Wyatt thought, looking around. It was beginning to look like a super-size block party. Kids were running around having a good time, their elders were knotted together in chatting groups and some folks had gotten folding tables from his garage and set them up as a buffet.

He held gatherings like this from time to time, but he'd never before had one create itself. Thank goodness he had a large house and yard. And out front, Gage and Jake had left the street blocked off, making it safe for everyone to cross and kids to run heedlessly back and forth.

"Don't you mind them biddies," the old man with

the cane said as he passed by with a plate full of sweets. "They don't influence anyone but themselves."

With a nod, he moved on.

"That was Harry Jenks, wasn't it?" Wyatt asked. While he knew almost everyone by sight after all these years, there were an awful lot of them, and apart from his friends he was mostly inclined to remember people who came before his bench.

"Believe so," Gage answered. "He was in town for some reason when he decided to join the party. You know his son, though. Keith Jenks, the rancher."

"Indeed I do. But I don't see Harry often."

"Doesn't come into town much anymore. I think he's glad he was here today."

Wyatt laughed. "I get that impression."

Gage faced him. "I know you have an election coming. I hope you're not worrying about it. It's in the bag, Wyatt. Folks think you're a good judge."

"Thanks, Gage, but I haven't been worrying about it, which seems to be driving my dad crazy."

Gage snorted. "Earl's good at that when it comes to you, I've noticed. Good thing he moved out of the house. You'd never have been able to breathe."

It was true, Wyatt thought. Earl had become a lot more enjoyable when they weren't sharing a roof, and while he still poked his nose into Wyatt's affairs, it wasn't nearly as bad as a few years ago.

Just as he was beginning to wonder if Amber had decided to sit this one out, she appeared on the back porch dressed in fresh jeans and a blue sweater. Before she could come to him, she got swallowed by a group of women he knew well: Hope Cashford, with a child on her hip, Julie Archer, swelling with her first pregnancy, and Ashley Granger, the fourth-grade school-teacher. The only ones missing from their little coterie were Connie Parish and Marisa Tremaine. A group of inseparable friends, they drew Amber in among them.

"Gage?"

"Yo?"

"Where's Connie? Is she on duty?"

"She got off forty minutes ago. Should be here soon. Why?"

Wyatt shrugged. "She and Ethan were on my guest list for tonight. Just a small gathering. She accepted, so I expected to see them."

"Small gathering?" Gage repeated. "That got all blown to hell." Then he gave his crooked half smile. "Now I gotta find out where my wife went." He limped away to look for Emma.

Wyatt circulated, pausing to chat briefly with everyone but working his way slowly around to Amber. At least she appeared to be enjoying herself. But that was a good group of ladies, and he'd hoped she might find some friendship with them. For however long she was here, she needed people besides him. That was just natural.

The cause of the party was nearly forgotten as everyone turned their attention to having a good time. Wyatt figured that was probably a good thing. Those women might have been a nuisance, but he didn't want anything stirred up against them. Sure, nobody much cared for that group, but most people were willing to live and let live.

He almost froze when he saw Ellie. What the devil? Why in the world would she have come here? He started to change directions, but she called out his name loudly enough that it carried over the conversations around him.

In an instant the cacophony quieted a bit, and he suspected people were waiting to see what happened. Slowly he turned.

"Ellie," he said quietly. Conversations in the immediate vicinity died even more. This was the downside of small-town life. There probably wasn't a person here who didn't remember him dating this woman.

He hoped she didn't make a scene, because he'd had quite enough. Her lies, those women out front, Amber being troubled by both Loftis's women and Ellie…yeah, he'd had enough. If she said the wrong thing, there were going to be words. Words he didn't want to say, because they were nobody else's business.

Just then, he felt an arm slip through his. Looking to the side, he realized that Amber had joined him and was smiling. "Hi, Ellie," she said. "It was nice of you to drop by the other day."

Oh, boy, Wyatt thought. *Here we go.* He saw the spark in Amber's gaze and understood that she was ready to go to battle on his behalf. Funny, he'd always seen himself in the role of protector, and now here she was assuming the mantle.

Reaching across his body, he laid his hand over Amber's, where it rested on his arm.

"Yeah, thanks for welcoming Amber to town, Ellie," he said. "I don't know if I ever told you, but we've been friends since law school. I've been looking forward to sharing my town with her."

Whatever Ellie had intended, he'd apparently defused it, because while her eyes narrowed, she said only, "Nice to meet you, Amber," then quickly moved away.

"Good job, buddy," said a familiar voice, and he turned his head to see Connie Parish. Quickly he introduced her to Amber, only to learn that Connie's other friends had already done so. "So, Wyatt, the gals and I want to take Amber out tomorrow afternoon, show her around a bit. After she feels better, of course. That okay?"

"Why wouldn't it be okay?" he asked, smiling. "I barely started introducing her to Conard City. I'm sure you gals can do a whole lot better."

"And enjoy some time away from family demands," Connie added wryly. She winked at Amber. "Pick you up around one?"

Amber smiled back. "That would be great."

As they resumed strolling through the crowd, stopping to pick up some finger foods, Amber said, "I feel like I'm surrounded by a squad of protection."

"You are," he answered. "You definitely are." And if he had anything to say about it, she was going to stay that way.

"This is a great party, Wyatt."

"Not exactly what I'd planned," he admitted.

"So I heard. But any place that can rustle up a potluck and party this fast…well, I'm impressed."

He caught her smile and saw that for the first time since she'd arrived, it didn't hold even a hint of shadows. For just this little while, Amber was free of everything and happy.

He just wanted her to stay that way.

Chapter Eleven

They made gentle love that night, very gentle, but Amber was tired and didn't take it amiss when Wyatt encouraged her to sleep.

It had been quite a day, she thought. She'd seen a lot of the city, she'd watched Wyatt defuse what could have turned into an ugly situation and there'd been a big party and even an encounter with Ellie.

As she drifted off to sleep, she appreciated just how interesting this town could be. And how full of surprises.

In the morning she was nauscated again, but it didn't seem quite so bad. She didn't have to go racing to the bathroom; just took her time eating crackers and sipping water until she felt she could rise.

Wyatt remained with her in case she needed anything, but when she felt over the worst, he headed downstairs to make breakfast and leave her to dress.

She thought over the day before again and actually smiled while she washed and donned fresh clothes. She wondered how much of a mess might be left downstairs. Everyone at the party had helped with cleanup, but she was sure at least some of the mess had been overlooked.

It had been fun. Much better than the formal parties she was used to attending, and she'd met loads of nice people who talked about things besides the law and business. This town was definitely growing on her, even the warts like Ellie and those women who had picketed Wyatt.

She almost giggled remembering it. Picketing him? Seriously? It seemed so extreme and so pointless. Truly over-the-top. And while she had at first been concerned for Wyatt, it had been no big deal for a lot of other people who had stayed to party. Just one of the quirks of this place.

Keeping in mind that she was going out with her new girlfriends that afternoon, she put on a good sweater and slacks. Truth to tell, she'd have loved to just stay here with Wyatt, but it would have been rude to turn down the invitation from the gals, as they called themselves. Besides, she shouldn't become too reliant on Wyatt. At some point she was going to need to go her own way.

Then she plopped on the bed as she remembered his proposal. He hadn't withdrawn it. But sitting there, she felt the urge to accept it growing stronger. That didn't seem fair to him. Didn't he deserve something better that a woman who was taking advantage of his protection? A woman whose career goals…

Oh, heck, what career goals? The last month or so

had given her plenty of reason to reconsider her entire future. She didn't want to go back to working for a big firm. Not anymore. So what did she want?

Maybe she owed it to herself and Wyatt to figure it out. Only when she was clear about that could she fairly decide such a momentous question for both of them. Or even just for herself.

She'd felt run over, smashed, by all that had happened. Then she'd turned her attention to just getting the hell out and away. Now she'd been here for a week, settling in, discovering that making love to Wyatt was even better than she had dreamed, but she still hadn't faced up to what lay ahead. She could either let life happen to her again, or she could make it happen.

Well, partly anyway. She knew that chance affected everyone in life, like the extremely remote chance that she would get pregnant while using birth control. But when you could take charge, you should. Not doing anything was a decision all by itself.

Wyatt had made some scrambled eggs with cheese for breakfast, and there was a stack of the inevitable dry toast if that was all she wanted. Given that her queasiness didn't seem quite as bad, she took a tablespoon of the eggs and tried them cautiously, aware that Wyatt watched her.

After she swallowed he asked, "Okay?"

"I think so."

He grinned. "Then dig in. I made plenty."

"So do we have much to clean up after last night?"

"Not a thing. My friends were especially nice, but the trash collectors are going to wonder at all the bags in the alley. Well, actually they won't, because they'll have heard if they weren't here." His dark eyes seemed to twinkle.

"People are going to hear a lot about yesterday, I bet." She glanced at him. "What in the world do you think Ellie intended to do?"

"I haven't any idea. Maybe nothing. Or maybe she decided that wouldn't be the best place to make a scene. It's even possible she's giving up her vendetta. It's probably hard to get anyone to listen after all this time."

She smiled, remembering. "You sure handled that smoothly. Your old friend from law school. Hard to come back with a stinger on that one." She looked at him again. "You handled all of yesterday wonderfully."

"I kind of had to, given that I'm a judge. It wouldn't have looked good if I'd erupted at those women and chased them down the street."

She bit her lip, holding in a smile. "Did you want to?"

"Hell, yes. Judicial temperament goes just so far. Underneath that robe is a mortal man, and I was angry. I don't care what they think of me, but I don't want them bothering you. Not at all."

She let the smile slip past her guard. "It was so over-the-top, Wyatt. Honestly, they didn't worry *me*. I was thinking about you but finding it so ludicrous. Who pickets for those reasons?"

"The Loftis gang. Gage got some of it two years ago when he was up for reelection."

"What in the world for?"

Wyatt shrugged. "They resurrected his old nickname. I told you. Hell's Own Archangel. That went away nearly a quarter century ago, but for some reason… I don't know what motivates them, Amber. Sometimes I think Loftis just stirs these things up to keep the group cohesive."

"Your dad advised me not to go to the pharmacy. He said he'd go for me if I needed anything."

Wyatt nodded slowly. "Or I will. Sometimes I'd like to put a gag on that man."

"Now that definitely wasn't judicial." She let laughter escape her and soon he joined her.

"The man behind the robe," he said in a deep voice, like an announcer. "His secrets, his failings, his…"

"Wonderfulness," she interrupted. "Of course you're human. I've seen some judges get pretty human on the bench. My favorite, though, was the one who snored his way through my closing argument."

"No!" He broke out laughing.

"Kid you not. I just kept going because I was talking to the jury anyway, and the bailiff looked almost frantic. He couldn't decide whether to wake the man or let him sleep. He probably figured he'd be in trouble either way."

"I hope not. Did you ever get an apology from the judge?"

"No, but he didn't need to apologize to me. I think the jury deserved that. Well, it *was* a boring case. The jury probably wished they could nap, too."

"Did it last long?"

"Weeks."

He nodded. "Even my longest-running cases rarely last more than a day or two. It's one of the reasons I like being a circuit judge. Always something fresh, even if I've seen it a hundred times before."

"Now that's a contradictory statement," she teased.

"But true. Different people make each case different, even if the applicable laws are the same."

"Unending soap opera?"

"Sometimes. Almost. I hope I never get so bored or burned out that I don't see the individuals, just the cases."

Then he paused and looked straight at her. "What about you? Are you settling? Feeling any better emotionally?"

After two nights in his arms, of course she felt better. But that wasn't what he was looking for, so she poked around inside herself, testing for the sore places.

"I'm not numb or furious anymore," she said slowly. "I'm not even sure I'm embarrassed that I was such a fool."

"Hard to be embarrassed by being conned when you look at what people were doing out in front of my house yesterday." He winked.

She laughed a little. "Point taken. I'm glad I came here. I spent a month stewing in my own juices, running around inside my own head and feelings. No room for anything else, and no room to start letting go. But since I came here... Thank you, Wyatt. It's all starting to feel different. I screwed up, but it's not the end of the world. Sometimes now I can even think about the baby and actually look forward to it. That's a big change in a week."

"I'm glad to hear it. Take as long as you need." He reached across the table and squeezed her hand. "The most important thing to me is that you find yourself again and decide what you want from life."

"Marriage?" she said lightly. At least she meant it to be light. Instead the one word seemed to suck all the air from the room.

His gaze grew intense, his hold on her hand tightened. "Are you proposing now?"

She pressed her lips together, suddenly in the midst of a whirlwind of uncertainty. Was that what she really wanted? He couldn't possibly be in love with her. He'd never even hinted at such a thing.

But as he'd said, there were other good reasons to marry, and love was no guarantee of success.

He didn't seem to expect an immediate answer, though. He released her hand and leaned back in his chair holding his mug of coffee. "I'm not pressing you. Take your time. But I'm also not withdrawing the offer."

How weird, she thought. Not bad weird, but still weird. He'd offered her marriage to take care of her and the baby, come what may, but the part that stuck in her mind was that he wanted a family. And from that she had understood that despite knowing hundreds of people around here, despite having an important and satisfying job, he felt lonely. What was missing? The intimacy of a live-in companion? A child?

She hesitated. "Your mother died when you were very young."

"Yeah." He tilted his head a little. "Are you going to psychoanalyze me? I'm sure it affected me, but it's not driving me. I made peace with it a long time ago."

He did seem awfully well balanced. Shaking her head a little, she sighed. She'd been too sheltered, she guessed. When life had decided to pull her shelters, it had done so in a big way all at once.

Now she was going to be a mother. Day by day, as she finally allowed herself to get used to the idea, that seemed to be the most important thing in her future. A mother.

What would have happened to Wyatt if he hadn't had a father to look after him? Gazing at him, she almost felt her heart stop. He was such a contained man. He had once referred to himself as staid, but she didn't see him that way at all. As he had said, he was human like everyone else, and she'd tasted some of his wildness when they made love the first time. She had also, over the years, seen flashes of anger in him, usually about an injustice. He felt, and felt deeply, but he didn't wear his heart on his sleeve.

So what had happened to make him so controlled? Certainly not simply the practice of law. No, he'd probably developed that a long time ago…maybe after his mother had died. He'd had to soldier on somehow.

She didn't want to pick at those scabs or demand he drop his guard. That wouldn't be kind. But she didn't think she was reading him wrong. Life had made him a rock. A rock she had leaned on before. A rock she was leaning on right now.

But a lonely rock. Did she make him feel less lonely? He'd said how nice it was to come home and find her there. Maybe it was the simple things he most lacked. Maybe that had prompted the proposal. Concern for her, certainly, but also a need of his own.

For the first time in a while, she was considering someone else's needs before her own, and she acknowledged once again that she had become quite selfish. Her parents had made her the center of their universe, and maybe in the process she'd started to think of herself that way. At least until she'd been scalded by life. The thought had entered her mind before, but now it was burrowing home painfully.

"Wyatt?" She spoke before she could stop herself. "I may be the most selfish person you know."

His eyes widened. "What do you mean?"

"My whole life has been about me until just recently. You couldn't possibly find that attractive." Not after what Ellie had done to him.

"I think you underestimate yourself."

"Really?" She waved a hand. "I've spent most of my life thinking about me."

He shook his head a little. "I think you've spent most of your life thinking about your parents. What they wanted. Anyway, that doesn't make you selfish."

"Sure it does. I moved myself and all my problems into the center of your life, upsetting everything, maybe risking your election. Did I ever once ask if this was convenient for you? I should have been able to take care of myself."

"Whoa," he said, a long, drawn-out breath. "Easy. Since you got here you've been worrying about me, even though it's not necessary. And if you remember, *I* was the one who suggested you come here. You never asked."

"No, I dumped. I didn't have to ask. I knew you'd come riding to the rescue if you could. That was unfair of me."

"So? You needed help. What are friends for? And I rather like the idea that you felt you could trust me to help. What kind of man would I be if I didn't?"

Well, she'd had experience of the other kind of man and didn't think that was a fair question. Maybe better to ask what kind of person he'd be. Silly quibble, though. As a lawyer with a love of very precise language, she had lately found herself in a place where that precision had little meaning.

She spoke, taking a risk, but needing to know. "What did you do in Afghanistan? I thought you were with the JAG?"

"I was, but not all cases happen here. I volunteered to investigate a mess involving some SEALs. They gave me some basic combat training before I went, but nobody expected things to blow up. Unfortunately they did." He made a gesture, as if pushing the subject away. "It's over and I'm fine."

Fine. "Kind of a wild thing to volunteer for."

"Someone had to do it." He shook his head. "It's a long time in the past."

Maybe so, but it told her more about him. Motorcycles and trips to dangerous places that he didn't want to talk about. He had his moments, too. That made her feel better. He wasn't perfect. But maybe most of his perfection had been created in her mind.

Thinking back she could remember his occasional impatience with people who made illogical legal arguments. He despised liars. It wasn't as if he hadn't shared frustrations of his own when they talked over the years. And some of his comments about one of the speakers at the last bar convention had been downright cutting.

So, okay, he was indeed human like everyone else. Somehow that eased her mind. What had she been doing? Turning him into some kind of superhero? Sheesh.

She could have laughed at herself. She looked across the table at him, feeling truly comfortable with him now, not inadequate in the way she had when she first arrived.

If she had been put through a blender in the last six weeks, she seemed to be coming out of it now. She was, indeed, settling down. Her mistakes didn't seem so big, and she no longer felt that surely Wyatt was way above her.

Obviously he didn't think so, but it was a little surprising to understand that she'd been harboring that feeling without recognizing it. He'd probably laugh if he knew, because she had learned that Wyatt didn't take himself that seriously. If he did, he wouldn't be wearing jeans and sweatshirts under his judicial robes. Ha!

She was so glad they had renewed their friendship, even if the circumstances weren't the best. Phone calls, emails, the rare meeting at a convention...none of those had served to cross the bridge of the years the way this week had. She finally felt as if they were meeting as equals, all the detritus from the law school years swept away. She no longer needed to see him as someone awesome and unattainable.

But she still thought he was pretty awesome. She smothered a giggle, because she didn't want to have to explain it to him. Didn't matter, anyway. When she'd needed a safe harbor, he'd welcomed her.

And now...now they could move forward, possibly together, possibly not, but he'd given her the space to become ready to take her first few steps in that direction.

Pretty amazing guy.

When the women came by to pick up Amber a while later, Wyatt waved goodbye from the porch then went back inside to his office. He had some work to do, but his thoughts kept straying to Amber.

He hadn't been fair to her by offering her marriage. He would have kicked his own butt if he could have. She needed to regain her strength and independence, not become reliant on him. Sure, it had seemed to make sense, and he wasn't going to withdraw the offer, but he'd feel better about it if she didn't decide it would be just an easy escape. He knew she'd thought of that. For one brief moment it had showed on her face. But only that once.

Thank God she hadn't leaped. This was one case where his help might have been harmful. He certainly ought to know better.

But by the same token he was a man of his word. He'd made an offer and said he wouldn't take it back. He just didn't want it to become a way to cripple Amber.

Sitting there, he had an urge to take his bike up into the mountains while Amber was out. Ride fast and ride hard to clear the cobwebs from his head.

Without another thought, he called Connie's cell and told her he was going to be out for a few hours. He'd leave the house unlocked for Amber.

After he disconnected, he thought he should give Amber a key. He should have done that when she first arrived. Shaking his head at himself, he ran upstairs to don his leathers and biker boots. Ten minutes later he and his bike were in the driveway. He put on his helmet and revved the motor.

The deep thrumming of that magnificent engine always satisfied him at some deep level. Moments later he was motoring carefully down the streets. Soon he was on a back road headed for the mountains, feeling free and happy, throwing caution to the winds.

As speed and dangerous curves forced him to concentrate on exactly what he was doing, his subconscious went to work. And out of nowhere he realized he might be making a mountain out of a molehill.

There was no reason that a proposal to Amber needed to be this complicated. He'd asked. She was an adult who could reach her own answer.

What he needed to do was stop worrying about all of it. He'd given Amber a haven, hers to do with as she pleased. He needed to drop his guard with her, and he just needed to settle back and enjoy whatever life brought his way.

Because it had brought something pretty amazing his way the past week.

"Just be grateful, jerk," he said, his voice bouncing back at him from his faceplate. *Just be grateful and let life flow.*

The girls introduced Amber to yet another member of their group, Marisa Tremaine, while they sat at tables that had been pushed together for them at the diner. Maude, the owner, was her usual grumpy self, but she didn't seem to mind the space the women took up, or the fact they were drinking bottomless coffee and tea. A different kind of friendliness, Amber realized. Maude's diner was evidently also a hangout.

Mostly she listened to the other women talk. They seemed so happy, laughing often and smiling constantly. They shared bits of their lives with complete comfort.

"Trace is back in DC," Julie Archer said at one point. "I wonder if he's ever going to be done with the hearings and investigation." She turned to Amber. "My husband still works at one of those alphabet soup agencies. He's trying to retire."

Marisa spoke. "Mine did, too, same agency. He managed to get away, though." She laughed quietly. "He's called Ryker, Amber. You'll like him."

As much as she liked all these women, she suspected she would like their husbands as well.

Ashley gave an exaggerated sigh. "I'm the only spinster among us now."

Julie grinned. "Maybe some alphabet soup guy will land on your doorstep, too."

"I can wish," Ashley said. She turned to Amber. "When you live in this place all your life, you know everyone. Or at least every eligible guy. I've tried most of them. Now I want a big surprise."

Amber had to laugh, because it was obvious Ashley wasn't really feeling sorry for herself. In fact, she said quite enough to convince Amber that she was happy with her life as it was.

"Tied up in a big bow," suggested Julie.

A peal of laughter escaped Connie. "Just make sure I don't have to arrest him for nudity."

Ashley giggled. "Actually, tied up with a bow sounds more like getting a dog. I'd like a dog."

"So get one," said Marisa, and soon they were discussing the relative merits of breeds and the possible complications of trying to work with no one at home to look after a pet.

"My kids want a dog," Connie said. "Begging constantly. But with Ethan and me both working? I don't know if that would be fair."

"A cat," suggested Marisa.

Amber listened, smiling, enjoying the free flow of conversation among these women. But all too soon they grew aware of the time and the need to get home.

"Next week?" they asked Amber.

"I'd love it."

Soon enough she was dropped off at the front door. Connie had told her that Wyatt had gone out but left the door unlocked for her. She climbed the steps, hoping he was home. His car was there, after all.

Just as she put her hand on the knob, however, she heard the distinctive rumble of a motorcycle coming down the street. She turned and saw a man in black leather riding a black Harley, his head totally concealed by a black helmet.

Oh, be still my beating heart, she thought when the bike turned into the driveway. Wyatt? She hoped so.

He brought the bike to a halt near the end of the porch and pushed his visor back. That was definitely Wyatt smiling at her. Her heart sped up immediately.

"Hey, Amber," he said easily. "Go on inside. It'll take me a few to park the hog."

She waited briefly, however, enjoying the sight of him until he maneuvered the bike into the garage. Only then did she go inside to await him. She even started coffee for him, figuring that if he'd been out riding for a while he might be a bit cold.

It was high time, too, she told herself, that she started helping with some of the chores around here. He cooked every breakfast, and she couldn't take that over as nauseated as she felt in the mornings, but maybe she could prepare a dinner or two when he was working the entire day?

Then Wyatt entered by way of a side door off the mudroom behind the kitchen, still in his leathers but without his helmet.

Her heart once again slammed into high gear as she spoke. "Do you have any idea how scrumptious you look right now?"

He grinned. "I like the sound of that. So leather turns you on?"

"When you're in it," she admitted.

His smiled widened and his eyes sparkled. "Then I'll wear it a little while longer."

Crossing the room and rounding the island, he said, "Do I smell coffee?"

"I'm making it…" Then before she could say more, he caught her beneath her bottom and lifted her. She reached for his shoulders for support, and the two of them met in a sudden explosion of fire.

He kissed her until she was breathless, then lifted his mouth from hers. "Our problem," he said huskily, "both of us, is that we put walls around ourselves and our feelings. Much safer that way."

Still partly dazed, she blinked, clinging to his shoulders, loving the feel of his hard body against hers. "What…when…"

"We need to talk," he said, slowly lowering her to

her feet. She hated it when he let her go. "Things just suddenly got very clear when I was riding. Coffee?"

She shook her head, waiting while he poured. Then she made her way to a chair, certain she wasn't going to like this at all.

Because when did *we need to talk* ever precede anything pleasant?

Chapter Twelve

He brought her a glass of milk, then asked if she wanted to stay in the kitchen or move to his office.

"Office," she said immediately. He'd made it a cozy, welcoming room, and for some reason she felt that whatever he wanted to say to her would be easier to take surrounded by books, old wood and comfortable chairs. Not here in the harsh edges of his modern kitchen.

He let her lead the way down the hall. She took the armchair she always used, set her milk on the side table and picked up his great-grandmother's shawl, spreading it over her lap, staring at its brilliant colors as if that beauty would save her somehow.

Instead of sitting behind his mahogany desk, however, he pulled the other armchair closer and sat facing her, cradling his coffee in his hands. She waited nervously, wondering what he had to say.

"I've been slowly realizing," he said, "that since Ellie I've been in a kind of emotional stasis. Hiding out so nothing like that will happen again. I think you started doing the same thing since Tom. What we feel…well, we'll never really share it unless we pull those walls down, Amber. In fact, I think both of us have been building those walls for a very long time. I'm honestly not sure Ellie ever got behind them, even though I considered proposing to her."

She nodded and swallowed hard. She couldn't deny it. All her life a big part of her had been locked away for whatever reason. Because she was so on task trying to please her parents. Because her need for success wouldn't let anything else get in the way. Until Tom.

"In my case," he said, "I closed up after Afghanistan. Mostly. There are parts of me I absolutely won't share. It's a self-protective shell. I need to stay objective, levelheaded…and not just because I'm a judge. I need it for myself."

She nodded again. Oh, did that sound familiar. "I let Tom get through and look where it got me."

He looked at her with a half smile. "Yeah, we both picked wonderful people to lower our barriers with. So as I was riding today I realized that I'm hunkered down in my fortress when what I really want to do is live. Not saying I don't want to stay here or be a judge, but I'm not letting anything else into my life. I'm not living a rounded life. And my proposal to you was like a business offer because I can't get around these walls, and yet I was reaching out for something I need. So I offered a merger, which must have offended the hell out of you."

"I wasn't offended," she said. "Did I say I was? But I *was* shocked."

"Of course you were. I've been kicking myself ever since I did it."

Her heart slammed. Here came the bad news.

"I didn't handle it well, and I'm not proud of myself. Not at all. My dad told you I was sweet on you back in law school."

"Yes." And she'd felt the same way. She looked down, running her fingers over the shawl. "I felt the same way, Wyatt. So don't be embarrassed."

"I'm not embarrassed. I just look back at those days and think I was a fool."

That jerked her head up, her heart racing. "A fool? You were never a fool."

"Yes, I was. Because I had all sorts of good reasons for keeping our relationship purely friendly, but I ignored the most important reason in the world not to."

She caught her breath. "Which was?"

"That I was in love with you. Instead of coming up with reasons why it couldn't work, I should have been fighting to find ways to make it work. But I didn't. I gave you up simply because I thought it was right for you."

"You never asked," she whispered, her heart climbing into her throat.

"No, I never asked you what you wanted or how you felt. Which makes me a complete ass, I guess. But I didn't. I went my way, you went yours and I tucked away a whole lot of what was in my heart because I had myself convinced it couldn't be."

"Oh, Wyatt…"

"When I think of that wasted decade, I feel like

a double fool. And maybe I'm wrong. Maybe you wouldn't have wanted me enough back then to risk your plans and future. I don't know and you can't possibly know. It's just that after this last week I got that you've always occupied a huge place in my heart. You're already inside my walls. I might as well open the gates and let you the rest of the way in. Unless you don't want it."

He stood up, walking around the room, amazingly handsome and attractive in his leathers. She wanted that image always seared into her mind, whatever happened.

And she wished she knew what to say. She was amazed that he was saying he'd always loved her. Had she always loved him? She knew she'd wanted him, that the desire for him had never faded entirely away. That phone calls and emails had never been quite enough to content her.

During this week, she'd seen the Wyatt she had grown to care about in law school, but she'd also seen the man he'd become. Impressive in every way.

"Anyway," he said, standing still and facing her, "you're free to do whatever you think is best for you. I just wanted you to know that my offer of marriage was nowhere near as loveless as I made it sound. I've always loved you, Amber. But I don't want an answer now. Marrying me would upend everything you've ever wanted."

Like she hadn't already done that? But she knew what he was saying. He wasn't going to leave this town nor would she want him to. She had to decide if she was prepared to make a life here with him, if she'd be content with it simply because she had his love.

Her heart was already swelling with her answer, but she withheld it, closing her eyes and trying to think rationally about something that in the end was going to be very irrational. But she owed it to both of them to be sure she wouldn't become discontented.

"I can work with your father?" she asked.

"Didn't he say so? He'd probably love a partner since I failed him in that respect."

A small-town law practice, the exact opposite of all her dreams. But those dreams seemed so fruitless now, so dry and pointless. A small-town law practice would never make her a federal judge, but from the way Wyatt talked it would also rarely be boring.

"And my baby?" she asked, her heart squeezing. Now that the child had become real to her, she had to think about it, too.

"Would be mine. It's yours. How could I not love it? Biology isn't everything."

She felt the last of her own walls beginning to crumble, and only in feeling them fall away did she realize how much of herself she'd been denying all these years.

Then she asked the question that burst the tension in the room and made him laugh. "Are you going to explain this to my father?"

It felt so good to watch him laugh like that, the sound rising deep from within him. "Yes," he answered when he caught his breath. "Pistols at dawn if necessary."

Then she laughed, too, and certainty began to settle into her own heart. She put the shawl aside and rose, walking over to him. When she reached for him, he welcomed her, wrapping her in his arms.

She gazed into his dark eyes and felt as if a load had lifted and only joy remained. "I love you, too, Wyatt. I think I always have. Who would have ever thought that I'd be grateful I met a cad like Tom?"

He laughed again, but not for long. This day had changed him. He looked young and exuberant again… just as she was feeling for the first time in forever.

Then he brushed his lips against hers. "Is that a yes?"

"Yes," she said firmly. "It's yes, and yes, and yes. How soon can we do it? Because now that my dreams are coming true, I don't want to wait."

"Your dreams?" he repeated. "Are you sure?"

"These are the real ones, not the ones I was given."

He smiled, then swept her away with his kiss, his touch, his loving.

They were married the following Saturday. Wyatt had planned to hold the ceremony in the clerk's office with the magistrate, a good friend of his, presiding. But in no time at all their small party of friends grew, and finally they had to move into the courtroom to actually take their vows.

"Like the potluck party," Amber whispered to Wyatt.

She was beaming, he noticed. Just glowing. She'd wanted nothing fancy or special, had reluctantly accepted the loan of a white dress from Julie Archer, over which she wore his grandmother's shawl, and she swore all she wanted was him. He couldn't have been happier and gazed at his lovely bride with amazement. God, she was beautiful inside and out.

The courtroom was filled to overflowing, but Wyatt forgot everything as he stared into Amber's eyes.

When he said his vows to her, his heart lifted until it felt like a balloon.

Over fifty of Wyatt's—and now Amber's—friends stood up to applaud when the marriage was completed, and they stepped out into a sunny, pleasantly cool late-October day to find that while they'd been inside the entire square had been festooned in white balloons and crepe paper streamers, and that another potluck had been marshaled by folks who had waited outside.

The number of people amazed Amber. She looked at him with a smile. "I'm touched. And I think you're pretty much a shoo-in for retention."

He smiled out at all the people as they came down the steps. "It kinda feels that way." He squeezed her hand where it lay on his arm. For once the judge was wearing a suit. "I'm sorry the honeymoon has to wait."

"I'm not. I've got a whole new life to discover."

So did he, he realized, watching her adjust his great-grandmother's shawl with her free hand. A whole new side of life, anyway. Marriage. Fatherhood. But mostly love.

The circle of their friendship had completed, and it was wonderful.

* * * * *

*Come back to Conard County in June 2017
for Ashley Granger and Zane McLaren's story
in Rachel Lee's next book in the*
CONARD COUNTY: THE NEXT GENERATION
miniseries from Harlequin Special Edition!

And catch up on previous installments:
AN UNLIKELY DADDY
A COWBOY FOR CHRISTMAS
THE LAWMAN LASSOES A FAMILY
A CONARD COUNTY BABY
REUNITING WITH THE RANCHER

*Available now wherever Harlequin books
and ebooks are sold!*

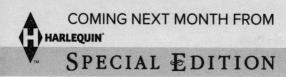

COMING NEXT MONTH FROM

HARLEQUIN®

SPECIAL EDITION

Available February 21, 2017

#2533 FORTUNE'S SECOND-CHANCE COWBOY
The Fortunes of Texas: The Secret Fortunes • by Marie Ferrarella
Young widow Chloe Fortune Eliot falls for Chance Howell, an ex-soldier with PTSD, but will their fear of another heartbreak stop them both from seizing a second chance at love?

#2534 JUST A LITTLE BIT MARRIED
The Bachelors of Blackwater Lake • by Teresa Southwick
Rose Tucker is a single woman with a failing business. Or so she thinks. Then her ex, Lincoln Hart, shows up with an offer for her design services...and the bombshell that a paperwork glitch makes them a little bit married.

#2535 KISS ME, SHERIFF!
The Men of Thunder Ridge • by Wendy Warren
Even as Willa Holmes vows not to risk loving again after a tragedy, she finds herself the subject of a hot pursuit by local sheriff Derek Neel. Can she escape the loving arm of the law? Does she even want to?

#2536 THE MARINE MAKES HIS MATCH
Camden Family Secrets • by Victoria Pade
Kinsey Madison has a strict policy about dating military men: she won't. Of course that means she can team up with Lieutenant Colonel Sutter Knightlinger to get his widowed mother settled and Kinsey in contact with her new family without risking her heart...right?

#2537 PREGNANT BY MR. WRONG
The McKinnels of Jewell Rock • by Rachael Johns
When anonymous advice columnist and playboy Quinn McKinnel receives a letter from Pregnant by Mr. Wrong, he recognizes the sender as Bailey Sawyer, his one-night-stand, and has to decide whether to simply fess up or win over the mother of his child.

#2538 A FAMILY UNDER THE STARS
Sugar Falls, Idaho • by Christy Jeffries
On a "glamping" trip for her magazine, Charlotte Folsom has a fling with her guide, Alex Russell. But back in Sugar Falls, they keep running into each other, and their respective families fill a void neither knew was missing. Will Charlotte and Alex be too stubborn to see the forest for the trees?

**YOU CAN FIND MORE INFORMATION ON UPCOMING HARLEQUIN® TITLES,
FREE EXCERPTS AND MORE AT WWW.HARLEQUIN.COM.**

HSECNM0217

Chance knew he should just go. Normally, he would have.
But something was making him dig in his heels and stay.
He wanted to get something straight.

"Is this the kind of stuff you're going to be feeding
those boys?" he asked. "Stuff about slaying dragons?"

"No, this is the kind of 'stuff' I'm going to be using
in order to try to understand the boys," she said. "To help
them reconnect with the world."

He laughed drily. Still sounded like a bunch of mumbo
jumbo to him.

"Well, good luck with that," he told her, shaking
his head. "But if you ask me, a little hard work and a
little responsibility should help those boys do all the
reconnecting that they need."

"Hard work and responsibility," she repeated, as if he
had just quoted scripture. "Has it helped you?" Chloe
asked innocently.

His scowl deepened for a moment, and then he just

waved her words away. "Don't try getting inside my head, Chloe Elliott. There's nothing in it for you. I'm doing just fine just the way I am."

She suppressed a sigh. "Okay, as long as you're happy."

Happy? When was the last time he'd been happy? He couldn't remember.

"Happy's got nothing to do with it," Chance answered. "I'm my own man on my own terms, and that's all that really counts."

He felt himself losing his temper, and he didn't want to do that. Once things were said, they couldn't get unsaid, and a lot of damage could be done. He didn't want that to happen. Not with this woman.

"I'd better go find the boss. Graham said that he wanted to take me around the spread as soon as I stashed my gear."

She didn't want to be the reason he was late. "Then I guess you'd better get going."

"Yeah, I guess I'd better." With that, he crossed back to the door.

He walked out feeling that there were things left unspoken. A great many things. But then, maybe it was better that way. He wasn't looking to have his head "shrunk" any more than it already was. Even if the lady doing the shrinking was nothing short of a knockout.

Some things, he reasoned, were just better off left alone.

Don't miss
FORTUNE'S SECOND-CHANCE COWBOY
by Marie Ferrarella,
available March 2017 wherever
Harlequin® Special Edition books and ebooks are sold.

www.Harlequin.com

#1 *New York Times* bestselling author

SHERRYL WOODS

**introduces a sweet-talkin' man to shake
things up in Serenity.**

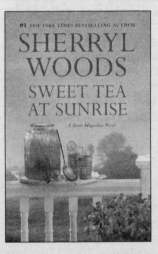

Emotionally wounded single mom Sarah Price has come home to Serenity, South Carolina, for a fresh start. With support from her two best friends—the newest generation of the Sweet Magnolias—she can face any crisis.

But sometimes a woman needs more than even treasured friends can provide. Sexy Travis McDonald may be exactly what Sarah's battered self-confidence requires. The newcomer is intent on getting Sarah to work at his fledgling radio station…and maybe into his bed, as well.

Sarah has learned not to trust sweet words. She'll measure the man by his actions. Is Travis the one to heal her heart? Or will he break it again?

Available now, wherever books are sold!

JUST CAN'T GET ENOUGH?

Join our social communities
and talk to us online.

You will have access to the latest
news on upcoming titles and special
promotions, but most importantly,
you can talk to other fans about your
favorite Harlequin reads.

Harlequin.com/Community

Facebook.com/HarlequinBooks

Twitter.com/HarlequinBooks

Pinterest.com/HarlequinBooks

THE WORLD IS BETTER WITH

Romance

Harlequin has everything from contemporary, passionate and heartwarming to suspenseful and inspirational stories.

Whatever your mood, we have a romance just for you!

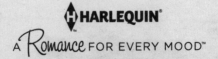